A QU
OF
GHOSTS

COMPILED BY
Aidan Chambers

THE BODLEY HEAD
LONDON

British Library Cataloguing
in Publication Data
A Quiver of ghosts.
1. Ghost stories, English
I. Chambers, Aidan
823'.01'08375 [FS] PR1309.G5

ISBN 0-370-31008-X

Printed and bound in Finland for
The Bodley Head Ltd
32 Bedford Square, London WC1B 3EL
by Werner Söderström Oy
First published 1987

Contents

The Black Prince

JOHN GORDON

If Arnold Duffield could have seen even a small distance into the future he would never have done what he did. He was changed utterly—by someone who said nothing to him but merely held his hand in silence. And Duffield was tough.

Until it happened, he enjoyed being envied for his Rambo muscles, which he kept oiled and ready for instant use. So he used them.

Claire had a blond fringe through which she admired him, although this did not stop her complaining. 'I don't see what we've come here for, Duffy,' she said. 'It's boring.'

Duffy was enjoying himself, although visiting a museum did not fit the image. 'You can blame your little brother,' he said. He pronounced it 'bravver', deliberately. 'It was him who wanted to come here.'

'Kids.' She pushed her lips forward, kissy and sulky. 'They're bloody boring.'

'I dunno what you mean about kids,' he said. 'You're only firteen.'

'So are you!'

'Yeh.' He spoke briefly. 'Yeh. OK.' But he knew he looked older than that. He glanced quickly around the long room. What he was enjoying about the museum were the exhibition cases themselves, not what they contained. It was all that glass. Ever since he had come in he had been clipping new magazines into the machine gun slung across his chest and stitching row after row of exhibits with bullets. The crashing cascades were too vivid in his mind to share with her. She didn't seem to like imagining things.

He stepped closer to the row of flat cases in the centre of the room. 'Come and look at this,' he said.

She went over to him, her hands pushed deep into the pockets of her short grey coat, and leant over the glass. 'That's only old bits of rock,' she said.

'Neat though, inni'?' he said. The pieces of coloured stone were each set in a shallow cardboard hollow and labelled. 'Must've taken ages to get right.'

'Yeah,' she said. 'Must've.' She looked at him sideways through her fringe. His face was close to the glass and he was so interested in what he saw he must have had a brain transplant or something. 'I'm beginning to wonder about you,' she said—just as the whole case tilted and the rock samples began to slide.

She gave a shriek, more of pleasure than fright, just as Duffy, with his forearms under the exhibition case, heaved again and the rocks rattled to the far side. 'What you do that for?' she said. 'Have you gone maid?' Duffy was strong on maidness.

'Nah.' He shrugged and pulled the cuffs of his bomber jacket down. 'I just wanted to stir fings up a bit, that's all.'

'Somebody'll come and stir you up, if you ain't careful.'

'What if they do?' He enjoyed seeing her giggle. 'I ain't worried.'

'You know what you are,' she said. 'You're a vaindal.'

'Well that's what this place wants—vaindalizing.'

Footsteps were approaching from the entrance hall. 'I'm getting out,' she said, and began to walk away.

'Chicken!' But he was speaking to her back. She had pushed her hands so hard into her pockets that it had

8

narrowed her waist and emphasized her bottom. He watched it retreating. 'Page Free,' he said, and sauntered after her just as a small man in a grey suit came in and stood by the doorway. 'This the way to the stuffed birds, Grandaid?' Duffy asked, nodding towards Claire as he followed her into the next gallery.

The man's face, shadowed by his glasses, stared after him, but he said nothing.

Mark heard the rattle of stones and his sister's laughter in the next room but he paid no attention. Neither did the dead woman, although her head was tilted slightly forward as though she was listening and had closed her eyes in order to hear better. Her face was brown and had shrunk so that her teeth were prominent, and she was propped upright in her coffin, still wrapped in the brown linen bands of her Egyptian funeral. One hand was exposed and rested against the wrapping, although it was so shrivelled it could have been a dried root that had grown through the ring that was welded by age to one of the fingers.

Mark turned away. Each time he came into the main hall he could not avoid looking at the mummy, but it was not his reason for persuading Claire to bring him here. You were supposed to have some older person with you in the museum, and there was something he badly wanted to see.

The high room had an arched skylight. Although no sky was visible through the crust of roof grime clinging to the glass, just enough light from the winter dusk outside filtered down to enable him to see what he had come for. He moved towards the exhibition cases that stood like a row of glass-topped tables along the centre of the floor.

He was small, even for eight, and he had to stand on tiptoe to see over the edge of the glass. What he saw was a jewel box so dazzling it always surprised him he was allowed to look into it without guards standing alongside him. It was better than diamonds.

Row after row of beetles shone under the glass. Even in this light some were as red and stared out as bright as a pheasant's eye, and some rippled with the blue of a peacock's neck. There were greens as fresh as apple peel, and there were studs of yellow like drops of new paint. Only the blacks seemed to be no more than burnt flakes waiting to be swept up. But then, in another room far away, switches clicked and lights sprang on in the gallery, and the blacks changed instantly. They took on a sheen of purple that was sometimes inside the blackness and sometimes hovering outside, the almost invisible cloak that was the oil of their armour.

Mark had a beetle of his own. He took its tiny cage from his pocket and rested it on the glass. The cage had begun as the tray of a matchbox but he had criss-crossed it with threads which he glued to the sides, and he had cut away one end and hinged it to make a door with its latch made from a bent pin. He undid it, and the Black Prince, a whole army of legs, marched out. He was not the largest beetle Mark had ever found, but he was the most friendly. He would always crawl on to his finger rather than run away, but now Mark gave him a clear run of the glass so that he could compare him with the others.

'In't it horrible?' Claire's voice was behind him as she came into the long gallery, but Mark knew she was not speaking about the Black Prince. He did not even look up. 'It in't hardly human, is it?' She was clinging to Duffy's arm as they went past the beetle case, ignoring it.

'His head's just like an old coconut,' said Duffy. 'Except for the teeth.'

'It ain't a he. It's a she.' She was reading the label. 'Look what it say—wife of a priest or suffin.'

'Yeah.' He leant forward in front of the woman. 'A woman, definite. She's showing off her wedding ring. I seen better at Woolworf's.'

Still clinging to his arm, Claire looked over her

shoulder. 'Duffy,' she said, 'listen.' The silence expanded outwards from room to room. 'There ain't nobody here but us.'

'What if,' he said, and paused so that she gripped tighter. 'What if one of them eyes suddenly opened? I think I just seen it twitch.'

'Shu' up!' She was clutching his arm with both hands, and the toes of her crinkle-top boots were pointed together.

'Don't take much to scare you, do it?' he said.

'I would never have come if it hadn't been for that stupid kid.'

They turned themselves around to look at Mark. He was gazing down through the glass and at the same time was shepherding his beetle back to its home. 'Come on, Prince,' he murmured.

'What's he say?' Duffy bowed his head closer to Claire.

'How would I know? He's always talking to himself.'

Duffy had his mouth open, listening to Mark, who was saying softly, 'Come on, Prince. It's time to go home.'

'Printh?' Duffy imitated Mark's lisp. 'What's he got? A bleedin' dog?' He went round the case, tugging Claire behind him, and towered over Mark. 'Woof-woof!' he said. 'Get down, Printh!'

The Black Prince had been a secret, and Mark's hands were trembling as he felt the beetle's legs tickle his fingertips. He eased the Prince into his cage and then, to distract attention, he pointed down through the glass. 'I think he's one of those,' he said. It wasn't exactly true, but there was a similarity between the Black Prince and the much bigger beetle pinned below with its head down and its back legs pushing at a ball of dung.

Duffy leant further over and read the label. Then he turned his big face towards Claire. 'You know what he's got?' She shook her fringe. 'You know what your brother's got in his hand? A shit beetle!'

Mark had not had time to properly secure the cage

door but now he covered the whole matchbox with his hand.

'I want to see one of them.' Duffy held his hand out. 'Let's have a gander.'

Mark shook his head.

Duffy mimicked fear. 'You in't going to set it on me, are you? Down, Prince! Down boy!' As Duffy shouted he slapped at Mark's hand and the cage flew across the floor.

'Look out!' Duffy's laughter was loud as Mark crouched to find the beetle. 'It might bite your hand off!'

The cage was face down, and Mark turned it over with feverish fingers. The door was open and the Black Prince had gone. He was searching the floor when heavy footsteps echoed in the room and a man's voice said, 'Out. All of you—out!'

The museum curator was not a tall man, and he seemed nervous. Duffy began to argue. 'We ain't done anyfing.'

'Out!' said the man.

'This place is open to the public inni'? We got a right.'

'Not when it's closing time, you haven't.' The man came closer and stooped over Mark. 'Are you with them, sonny? It's time to go.' He spoke more kindly, but Duffy was still jeering.

'You want to be careful, mister. He'll set his beetle on yah! Down, Prince!' He was already swaggering out, well enough satisfied with his performance in front of Claire.

The man pulled Mark to his feet. 'No playing about in here,' he said.

'I'm not playing.' But it was too late to explain; he was pushed after the other two.

In the street outside, Duffy continued to jeer, but the curator gazed down at them without a word and shut the door.

'Little Hitler!'

Claire was already moving away. 'He'll find them rocks in a minute,' she said, 'and then he'll be after you.'

Mark, with tears on his cheeks, spun round. 'And I hope he gets you!' he yelled. 'I hope you get put in prison!'

'Snivellin' little git!' Duffy raised the back of his hand, but Mark drew away from both of them.

'I ought never to have listened to that stupid kid,' said Claire. 'Him and his bloody beetles.'

Mark looked at the cage in his hand. A street lamp made shadows inside it, but there was no Black Prince. 'I hope you both go to prison!' he shouted, but Claire made a move towards him and he turned and ran.

'Good riddance!' she said to his back, but an hour later she wished she had held on to him.

'You were supposed to be looking after him,' said her mother. 'You should never have let him out of your sight in the dark.'

'I couldn't help it.' Claire had a whine that could quickly turn to anger. 'You know what he's like. He just ran off.'

'Just you be quick and eat your tea!'

The kitchen was bright and warm, but Claire's father did not have a chance to enjoy it. He said very little when he came home from work. He merely listened and then went back into town to look for Mark. It was his silence that made Claire think again.

'Dad's bound to find him,' she said.

Her mother's face remained grim.

'It's not as though it's a very big place, is it, Mum?' She knew Mark would be among the alleyways around the market place. That was the way he had run off. But then she had another thought. The river was not far away. 'He'll be all right,' she said.

Her mother did not reply, and Claire could eat no tea.

Once he had crossed the market place, Mark doubled

back. His eyes were watering, but not with tears. It was becoming very cold as the night came on.

There were parked cars in the road where the museum stood, but it was a back way and the pavements were deserted. He looked up the flight of steps to the museum entrance, and through the glass panels in the upper half of the door he could see the lights still burning. The clock on the church around the corner chimed the third quarter. He still had time.

He climbed the steps and peered inside. The entrance hall was empty, and beyond it he could see into the first gallery. Nothing moved. He was sure there could have been no more visitors; it was too late. But there was still the curator. He must be lurking somewhere, ready to emerge as soon as the door was opened. It was too risky. Mark had begun to back down the steps when he saw that there was still a chance. A window to the left of the doorway showed an office with tall filing cabinets, and the curator was there, his head bowed, working at a desk.

The brass handle was icy but turned easily, and the door swung silently inwards. Mark stepped on to the thick doormat and eased the door shut. It was very quiet. He stepped from the mat to the brown lino, and the soles of his trainers squealed. He stopped, ready to turn and fling himself out and away down the steps. From behind the office door came the sound of papers being turned over. He waited for it to cease suddenly as the curator, sensing that somebody was nearby, raised his head, listening. But the rustling continued.

Mark raised himself on his toes and, with a slow, rocking step, moved forward.

In the first gallery, the lamps high overhead shone with the deserted light of a forgotten castle, and he skirted the wall like a mouse until he came to the arch leading to the next room. A yellow stillness in the long gallery was reflected back from the walls of glass cases,

14

and the lamps hung on cords so long the domed ceiling was in shadow.

Now he was out of earshot of the office he moved quickly until he saw that the polished lino was pitted with little marks. Any of them could have been the Black Prince and he trod carefully, bending over, but none of the specks was a beetle. He crouched at the spot where the cage had been struck from his hand and peered beneath the exhibition case. The lino covered only the gangways, and here it was bare floorboards. The Prince could be anywhere in the cracks, in a strange land without friends. Mark crawled into the shadows and was sweeping the floor with his hands when a sound from the foyer made him stop. A door had opened, and hollow footsteps sounded in the museum.

'Five minutes!' It was the curator's voice. 'Five minutes to closing!'

He was calling out as he made his rounds, and it was obvious from the speed with which he marched from gallery to gallery that he knew the museum was empty. Mark could not see his top half, but he saw the walking legs and was waiting until they went by so that he could slide out from his hiding place and run for the foyer when, across the walkway, he saw a tiny movement. A beetle crawled at the foot of the exhibition cases.

The grey trousers and the feet moved away. A shutter clattered across a window and a bolt was shot to. The curator's back must be towards him.

Mark eased himself forward just as the beetle, testing the air with its antennae, began to scuttle away. Somewhere behind him, the curator was moving, but walking away, leaving the gallery. Mark crawled into the open and reached out for the beetle. His finger was on the point of touching it when the lights overhead suddenly went out. There was a moment when the gallery was filled with slanting shadows from the lights through the archway, and then these also flicked out, and next

15

the distant lights in the foyer. Almost instantly, far sooner than Mark expected, the outer door opened and banged shut. The museum was closed.

'Prince!' He whispered towards the floor, feeling with his fingers. 'Prince!' As soon as the familiar tickling touched him he would cup his hand over the beetle and make for the door. His shouts would bring the curator back.

Once he thought he felt it, but his fingers closed on a nail head. He swept the floor gently, calling on the Black Prince as he did so, but he knew that in the dark it was useless.

Sometimes, when he was in bed with the cage on his pillow, he could hear the Prince's six legs scratching as he walked. Perhaps he would be able to hear it again in the huge silence that surrounded him. He sat on his heels and listened. There was empty air behind him, and in front. No light came from the shuttered windows, and the skylight was no more than a wavering patch high overhead, but it shed its grains of greyness to where Mark crouched motionless.

Slowly his eyes gathered enough light to see shapes within the cabinets. First there was the lid of the mummy case. The patterns painted on it made it darker than the open coffin alongside it, but as he strained his eyes he saw the dimness that could only be the ancient, overlapping bandages. He did not make out the shape of the head until it moved.

The night was terrifying. Boats dragged the river and policemen with torches hunted behind bags of rubbish in dark back alleys. All night long Mark's father called on neighbours and searched their gardens, and his mother kept watch at home, fully dressed, tightening a handkerchief around her fingers until it bit them, as though this could hold her little boy in this world. Claire wept herself to sleep for a few sickly hours.

The curator had the most unpleasant shock of all. It was raining next morning as he climbed the steps to the front door of the museum and he had his hat pulled low so that his key was already reaching for the lock before he saw the face through the glass panel.

'He was simply staring at me,' he told the police. 'Looking at me with those great big eyes in that pale little face. I thought . . . I thought, I don't know what I thought. And his hands were so white against the glass they didn't look alive.'

But Mark was alive and wrapped in a policeman's coat.

'Thank God,' said the curator. 'Oh son, why didn't you let me know you were there last night?'

'I don't know,' said Mark, and looked at somebody else.

All day he had to keep looking away from people because whenever they spoke to him they wanted to know too much. Hiding in a museum just to find a beetle, and then to remain there until morning would not make sense to them, so he did not mention it. Nor did he tell them what else had happened during the long night. He said nothing about it even to his father who had tears on his face when they met, nor to his mother who only wanted to touch him, again and again.

Claire was the only one that day who wished him to remain quiet. She wanted nobody to know of her part in it. And later on, when the questions became too persistent and he began to speak, she kissed him for telling a lie. He said he had dropped some money in the museum and had gone back to look for it, but then had been too frightened to try to raise the alarm and eventually had fallen asleep.

Nobody knew about the Black Prince until more than a week later. It happened in a bus shelter, and Mark would never have been there with Duffy and Duffy's mates if it hadn't been for Claire. Ever since the night he had gone missing she had been told to meet him from school and bring him home, but the task was becoming a drag, so she went out of her way to meet the others at the shelter.

'Here she come, Duffy,' said a pale, lanky boy, taller even than Duffy himself. 'Got a kid taggin' along.'

'Mary had a little lame,' said Duffy. He bleated like a sheep, but his thin friend had embarrassed him and he turned on Claire. 'Proper little muvver, incha?'

'Well, whose fault is that!' She had a short temper, and her own head jerked forward, spitting the words at him.

'This the kid that got in the paper?' said the lanky boy.

'Little git,' said Duffy.

'He must be a bit thick, ain't he, Duffy—chuckin' his money on the floor and then spendin' all night lookin' for it.'

'Oh, no, he's not stupid!' Claire rounded on the thin boy, then stabbed a finger at Duffy. '*He*'s the stupid one!' And then the whole story of how the beetle cage was knocked to the floor came out.

Duffy laughed. 'He calls it Prince!' he said. 'Prince!' He barked like a dog.

There was a shout of laughter from everybody except the pale boy. He seemed to be thinking of something else. 'Tell you what, though,' he said when the noise subsided, 'I wouldn't want to be in there by meself all night.'

'Nothin' to it! Not if you're stupid enough to have a beetle for a pet.' Duffy barked again. 'He just fell asleep, that's all.'

'No, I didn't!' Mark had not meant to say anything. He just wanted to go home. Now they were all looking at him.

'What you mean?' Duffy glared. He allowed nobody to challenge him. 'The paper said you went to sleep—and it was you who told 'em.'

'I was awake,' said Mark.

Claire shuddered. 'You never was, was you? Not with

them things all around you. I would've gone out of me mind, I know I would.'

Mark did not want to be a hero. It would only make them sneer. 'A lady came,' he said. 'She had beads in her hair.'

'What lady? You never said nothin' about a lady.'

'She was nice,' he said. 'She had a white dress.' It was long and touched the floor. And he remembered her very dark, wide eyes. 'She helped me find my beetle,' he said.

'Heel, Prince!' Duffy was again greatly amused, and all the others laughed with him, except one.

'Did you?' said the pale boy. He alone seemed not to be afraid to speak across what Duffy was doing. 'Did you find it?'

Mark nodded. The woman had skin that was dark and smooth, and her hands were long and thin. He remembered the ring on her finger and the way, when she had crouched down beside him as though it was natural to her to rest that way, she had stroked the ground with her hand, and the Black Prince had come straight to her palm.

'Show us the beetle, then. Let's see it.' Duffy's face frightened him, but Mark shook his head. This was a mistake, because it could only mean that he had the Black Prince with him, and suddenly Duffy darted forward and dragged Mark's hand from his windcheater pocket. The matchbox cage was in his fingers and Duffy tried to prise it free. Mark clung, and Duffy's big fist closed over his and squeezed. He did not have the strength to prevent it, and he felt the cage crumple inside his own hand.

'You didn't ought to have done that.' The pale boy's eyes were on Duffy.

'Why not?' Duffy stood back, grinning. 'Little git's a liar as well. He had it all the time.'

One or two haw-hawed with him as they watched Mark open his fingers. He tried to straighten the crushed wreckage, but it was useless. The Black Prince was broken and dead.

'Just look what you done!' The shout came from Claire, and it was directed at Duffy. But it was the boy with the pale, raw face who spoke. He was looking at Mark.

'You ain't cryin',' he said.

Mark shook his head. Not yet.

'He ain't cryin'.' The boy's eyes lifted from Mark and rested on Duffy.

'Well, he don't have to, do he? Not over a bloody beetle.'

'Seems to me he don't cry a lot anyway,' said the boy. 'Not even when he get shut up all night.'

'There wasn't much use cryin' then, was there?'

'No, Duffy. But some of us would.'

Duffy's grin vanished. 'Meanin' who?' he said.

The boy shrugged.

'Meanin' me?'

There was a nervous snigger from one of the others, then silence. The pale boy stood quite silently.

'Meanin' me?' Duffy was in a boxer's slouch, but it was Claire who answered.

'Meanin' you!' she cried. 'You're scared, Duffy! You couldn't do it.' She put an arm around her brother's shoulder. 'Mark can, but you can't!'

Duffy tried to make a joke of it. 'I ain't got no beetle to find, have I?'

He was grinning, but it was too late. Nobody laughed. 'I should get seen,' he said. 'And I should get chucked out after what I did to them rocks.'

'Not if we all went together.' Claire was deadly. 'We could get you in, and Mark could show you where he hid.'

There was silence. Duffy sneered and turned away. In

a moment he would be in the clear because nobody was going to seriously challenge him.

Even the pale boy seemed out of it. His eyes had never left Mark, and now he said quite quietly, 'He still ain't crying.'

'So what?' said Duffy.

'So could *you* do what he done?'

There was no getting out of it now, and Duffy knew it. He led the way and, when they had all crowded into the museum, he was in the middle.

It was the first time the curator had seen Mark since that rainy morning a week ago, and he paid small attention to the others.

'Young man,' he said, 'I hope you're not going to give me another fright.'

'No,' said Mark. 'They just want to see where it happened.'

'It's nearly closing time,' said the curator. He was smiling, thinking back to what had happened. It had caused a bit of a stir in his quiet backwater, and there had even been a noticeable increase in winter visitors to the museum. The business of the disturbed stones had been pushed from his mind. 'He's a brave kid,' he said to the jostling crowd, 'but just you be careful you don't leave him behind this time.'

'We won't, don't worry.' Claire clung tightly to Mark's hand, and even though the curator was never far away it was easy for Duffy to slide beneath the exhibition case without being seen. His courage seemed to have returned, and he crouched down smiling. But Mark knew why. He could see the cunning in his face. All that Duffy had to do was make a noise as the curator went on his rounds and he would be discovered and turfed out.

It was Mark who lingered, holding Claire back as the others made a good job of distracting the curator's attention before they wandered towards the door. The curator, shepherding them out, paused beside Mark.

'You're the one I've got to make sure about,' he said.

Mark looked up at him. 'I'm last again,' he said.

'So you are.' The curator found it difficult not to laugh.

'Can I do something?' Mark asked.

'And what might that be?'

'Could I switch the lights out, please?'

The curator was amused. Duffy heard him laughing as he said, 'Very well, young man. I suppose you want to see what it's like to be in the dark again.'

Mark nodded, and for the first time he smiled. The curator would make no rounds in the dark.

Duffy heard a jumble of footsteps, a pause, the click of light switches, and darkness clamped him on every side. Only the thought of Claire being there to witness what happened kept him where he was. Otherwise he would have walked out with any excuse and relied on his fists to keep the others quiet. But that would never work with Claire.

There was still a chance to give himself away accidentally. He shuffled his feet on the floorboards.

The curator continued to chatter in the foyer.

Duffy kicked the leg of the exhibition case.

The echo he made in the gallery was answered by the dull thud of a distant door.

There was a rattle as the curator, on the steps outside, tried the handle and Duffy's hopes rose. The curator was coming back for something—surely he must be.

Duffy held his breath, listening. The rattle ceased and there was no sound of a door opening. Silence and darkness sat together, his only companions in the empty museum.

The kid had done this. Hatred of that young oval face and the large eyes that never seemed to blink made him snarl at the floor. And that bloody kid had fallen asleep just here. Duffy dug his nails into the floorboards. The effort warmed him. That was the way to get through the night. Hate would do it.

He clawed at the hard floor as though he was a lion tearing at that kid. That stupid kid and his bloody beetle. So bloody stupid he had gone to sleep. No. Not sleep. Duffy struggled to keep out of his mind the other thing. The lady. That stupid bloody kid's stupid bloody dream. With beads in her hair. He ripped at the floor with his claws, fighting to tear the picture from his mind.

And he succeeded. The image was shredded by his rage, and he crouched, panting.

Now that he knew how to give himself courage, he ceased to be afraid. He let out his breath, loudly.

There was an echo. Very faint, but it took a long time to die, whispering away from him as he held himself still. Then there was silence.

He was about to draw in his breath, when the sound came again of its own accord, stealthily, as though someone else was attempting to breathe in time with him. And he knew what was happening. One of the others had stayed behind. Some bloody idiot wanted to scare him, make a fool of him.

He pinpointed the sound. It came from near the shadowy glass case in the corner of the room. Keeping it in view, he slid into the gangway, and as soon as he was in the open he shouted.

'I know you're there!'

The echo of his voice was swallowed by the gaping halls. And the sound came again.

'Come out!'

He used all the power of his lungs.

'Come out!'

And then he saw that he had been heard. Within the glass case in the corner, something was shifting, slowly and softly obeying his order. It was coming out.

His rage left him, and his courage sank through the floor. He shrank down until he knelt in the gangway, making himself small, wanting to whimper but afraid to breathe. He was alone. There was empty space around and behind him, darkness through which a mist of light filtered. He saw the soft shine of the gangway stretching away in front of him until it reached the tall face of the exhibition case in the corner.

The sound was like air expelled between teeth. But nothing was breathing. It was a door moving. A glass door. He saw it swing outwards, and a sensation of dryness, a delicate, ancient odour reached him. The shape from the mummy case stepped so slowly he could have walked away ahead of it. But he remained where he was, his limbs locked tight, and the stuffed birds in the glass case behind him looked down from their branches.

Duffy moved his head. It was the bravest thing he had ever done. Mark's lady had worn white and had beads in her hair. He tilted his head to look up at her.

The figure that shuffled forward scraped the ground with mummy cloth, and the head that nodded as it came wore nothing but the flat ringlets of dead hair. Its eyes were closed, and remained closed as the cloth rustled and folded and the shape crouched beside him. One hand showed. It reached out for him, found his hand, and curled its fingers around his.

The brittle touch was gentle, almost soft, like thin leather, except where the ring and its emblem, the scarab beetle, dug deep. And held.

The Silver Box

LOUISE LAWRENCE

There was nothing special about number Forty Seven. It was indistinguishable from all the other houses in Gossington Square, part of a Victorian terrace divided into flats, its stone façade showing signs of decay. Rooms were big and gloomy and full of draughts, and during the day most of the residents were out. Carole took a throat lozenge from the silver box, sat on the window seat and watched the snow. Lime trees at the centre of the Square looked black against the whirling whiteness and the street was empty of traffic and people. Except for Carole the house was empty too . . . everyone away at work . . . her mother teaching at the comprehensive school . . . Mrs Dawkins from downstairs helping in the Oxfam shop . . . and the man from the basement gone to his office. And overhead the attic flat was once more unoccupied. Someone had died there, Mrs Dawkins claimed. A housemaid whose sweetheart had been killed in the First World War had committed suicide, and no one stayed for very long. Carole did not believe in ghosts, but the house creaked with stillness and the silence oppressed her. She was sick of being alone.

She had glandular fever, the doctor said. It was caused by a virus and was slightly contagious so she should not return to school until after Easter. Now it was January and Carole had nothing to look forward to for the next three months but Paracetamols and a pain in the neck, headaches and fatigue and feelings of grottiness, and a fluctuating temperature that made reality look strange. Perspectives were unstable. Walls seemed either too near, or too far away. The floor had a slope to it and the wind rattling the window got on her nerves.

Carole shivered and returned to bed. A sensible move, except that most of it was occupied by a fat black and white cat. Officially Splodge belonged to Mrs Dawkins and was there on loan to keep Carole company until Mrs Dawkins returned at one o'clock to prepare the lunch. But all he ever did was sleep, warm and heavy in the place where her legs ought to be. 'Shove over, you great dozy beast!' Carole said irritably. Green eyes opened, glared at her in annoyance, before he curled and settled again in the crook of her knees. When Splodge was sleeping, Mrs Dawkins said, he did not like to be disturbed. And in consideration Carole was trapped there for the rest of the morning.

Lonely and boring, the hours stretched endlessly ahead. She might have switched on the radio or studied her school books, but listening to music made her headache worse and she could not concentrate. Curled with the cat she tried to sleep but then she grew hot and sweaty and small sounds distracted her . . . the whine of the wind down the boarded-up chimney, the flutter of snow against the window pane, and the creak of a floorboard. It was as if someone were there, quietly moving at the far end of her room. Carole raised her head. She saw nothing unusual . . . just a shimmer of heated air above the electric convector heater and the walls receding into distances, the effects of her fever. But the sounds went on, movements and footsteps, soft and disturbing. And did she imagine the room was growing dark?

There was a humming noise too, like high frequency static almost beyond the range of her hearing. Once more Carole raised her head and for one panic-stricken moment she thought she was going blind. There was light around her bed but the rest of the room had vanished, dissolved in a curtain of shimmering air and darkness beyond it. Or maybe something was wrong with the convector heater? The electronic hum was clearer now, increasing in pitch. Even the cat could hear it. And they moved together, Carole and Splodge, propelled by the same fear. He rose from the bed with green eyes blazing, arched and spat and bolted for the door, his tail bushed as a fox's brush . . . and she switched off the convector heater and made to follow.

But the humming noise ceased and the shimmering grew steady, hung as a veil of sheer air from ceiling to floor, and beyond it the room was still there. Carole paused to stare, her curiosity conquering her fear. It was as if she were seeing into another world. It was morning where she stood but there it was night. A full moon shone through a broken window and trees in leaf made flickering shadows on the floor. She could smell warmth and flowers and sweet summer air, and in the room a smell of musty decay. She sensed, rather than saw, that time had changed. The house was old. Paper peeled from the walls, the ceiling sagged and the floorboards rotted. It was long ago, thought Carole, or maybe not. She noticed wires and cables, arc lights and cameras and video-recorders, computer terminals and electronic equipment. It was as if her room had been turned into a television studio or the set for a horror film.

Unless she was dreaming?

'Hold it!' said a voice.

'What now?' asked another.

'There's a definite energy reading here.'

'It's probably a rat.'

'Just let me check.'

Suddenly someone appeared beyond the wall of wavering air. For all it was dark at that end of the room Carole could see him quite clearly . . . a boy in a black cat-suit, his fair curls blowing in the wind. She saw the silver shine of his wrist-watch, slim limbs and the flash of his smile. And through him she saw the window frame, the moon through his face, the stars behind his eyes. He was there and yet not there. Beautiful, she thought, and as transparent as a ghost.

'Hey, Zak!' he said excitedly. 'Come and take a look!'

'No way, screwball!' the other replied. 'I'm not falling for that.'

'This is for real, Zak. We've actually got one!'

'A grey rat or black?'

'A girl standing by an antique bed. She has long brown hair and is wearing a floral nightdress buttoned to the neck. It's pink and old-fashioned and she's very pale. We've done it, Zak!'

'Bullshit!' Zak replied.

He too came suddenly into view . . . another ghost, big and bearded and bespectacled, scruffy as a student, with some unreadable slogan printed on the whiteness of his T-shirt. By his accent Carole guessed he was American and although he stared directly at her she had the peculiar feeling he was unable to see her, that in some way she was invisible. His words confirmed it.

'You're imagining things, buddy.'

'What do you mean?' the fair one asked.

'There's nothing there but the wall.'

'Don't be ridiculous! She's as clear as day!'

'Are you bullshitting me, Matt?'

'No,' Matt said earnestly. 'I'm telling you, Zak. Believe me . . . she *is* there.'

Carole was there all right. She had long brown hair and was wearing a floral nightdress just as Matt had described. But Zak saw no one and nor was he about to be convinced. The experimenter influenced the experiment, he said, and Matt was seeing what he wanted to see. His own hyped mind had produced the energy reading, *and* Carole. She was a mental projection, not a genuine phenomenon. Matt shifted the tripod and set up the camera. Seeing was believing, he retorted, and he believed Carole was real. And on heat-sensitive film her outline was bound to show. She watched him in annoyance. He did not behave as if she were real. He did not ask permission or ask if she minded, explain who he was or what he was doing there.

'Smile please,' he told her.

And something snapped.

'Get out of my bedroom!' Carole said. 'You've got no right to come barging in here and take my photograph! Who the hell do you think you are?'

Matt seemed to freeze in the flickering moonlight.

Then clutched Zak's arm.

'Did you hear that?' he said.

'What?' asked Zak.

'She spoke.'

'Leave it out!'

'I'm telling you, Zak. Who the hell are we, she said.'

It was a peculiar meeting . . . Matt in the midnight darkness and Carole in the morning light with the veiled air shimmering between them. His full name was Matthew Boyd-Hamilton with a hyphen, he said, and Zak was over from the United States on a two-year student exchange. They were both studying parapsychology at the nearby university and Carole was vital to their experiment. She did not understand the technicalities of time displacement and psychokinetic traceability, but she agreed to take part. After all, Matt was very good-looking even if he was a ghost, and talking to him was better than being bored and alone.

'So what do you want me to do?' she asked him.

'Scientifically,' he said, 'we need to prove you exist.'

'Isn't it obvious?'

'To you and me, maybe. But say-so isn't enough. It's not enough to convince Zak, let alone the board of examiners.'

'So what do you want me to do?' Carole repeated.

Zak, who was an electronics expert, set up the equipment and ran through a series of tests. Portable computers flickered and buzzed but apart from the original bleep of the energy pulse Carole failed to register. Nor did she show on the heat-sensitive video-camera, in infra-red or ultraviolet light. Except to Matt she remained invisible and inaudible, her existence unproven. In other words, said Zak, she was not really there.

'Are you calling me a liar?' asked Matt.

Carole took a throat lozenge from the silver box and waited while they argued. Whatever Carole was, said Matt, a mental projection or an independent entity, they needed to find out. And when high technology failed, human minds came into their own. Zak's machines were not infallible. And what was wrong with a tape recorder and common sense? If they could verify whatever information Carole gave them . . .

'If,' said Zak.

'It's worth a try,' said Matt.

'Would you like a blackcurrant throat sweet?' Carole asked.

'No!' said Matt . . . then turned towards her, as if he suddenly remembered she was there. 'No thanks,' he said. 'If you touch the circuit you'll probably break it and we're not into experiments of telekinesis.'

'What's she saying?' Zak asked suspiciously.

'She says . . .'

Matt hesitated, regarded Carole thoughtfully, as if for a moment he too doubted her reality or else she had no right to be chewing sweets in his company. She closed the box, saw his eyes following her movements, the pressure of her fingers on the hinged lid.

'What's wrong?' she asked him.

'Nothing,' he said.

'That's what I mean,' said Zak. 'If everything she says is inaudible it's not going to work, is it?'

But it did work. For the benefit of Zak and the tape recorder Matt repeated everything Carole said. It was very mundane, just details of her name and age, where and when she had been born, which Zak intended to check with the Central Records Office. And even that much seemed questionable, as if the date of her birth was not as they had expected. She had to produce the calendar for confirmation. She had been born sixteen years ago, she insisted, and now it was 1987 . . . January 21st 1987. Outside it was snowing . . . Mrs Thatcher was Prime Minister . . . and why on earth should she remember the First World War?

'Zak?' said Matt.

'Yeh,' said Zak. 'I heard.'

'Someone's goofed. Your time displacement machine has got to be faulty.'

'How about your imagination, buddy?'

'If I were making her up she'd fit the preconceived image,' argued Matt. 'She'd have a mop and a feather duster and the date would be 1917. Right? That means . . .'

'OK!' said Zak. 'That *suggests* she's genuine, existing in her own right and nothing to do with you. But *if* she's genuine how come I don't see her? And how come on all this psycho-sensitive equipment she doesn't show?'

Matt shook his head. The moon was gone and infrared light made all things colourless, stripped him of clarity and dissolved him to a shadow, as if he were hardly there at all. And Zak too was no more than a grey shade restlessly prowling, checking and re-checking the vision screens and print-outs, leaving his footprints on the dusty floor. He made Carole feel responsible, as if she ought to apologize for being what she was. Instead she shivered, not knowing what to say.

The room had grown cold without the convector heater. She could feel the chill of the night wind through

31

the broken window and Matt's eyes watching her, intense and curious, as she reached for her dressing gown. It was pale blue quilted, she heard him tell Zak, and she was obviously sensitive to temperature, reacting to her own space-time environment. And now she was taking a blackcurrant throat lozenge from a silver box . . . similar to a box his mother had at home on her dressing table which had been handed down through the family.

'You want me to go on?' asked Matt.

'No,' growled Zak. 'I've heard enough!'

'But it's odd, don't you think?'

'You ought to be on stage, Boyd-Hamilton!'

'Two blackcurrant lozenges in half an hour . . . why should I imagine that?'

'I've got glandular fever,' Carole told him.

'She says she has glandular fever,' said Matt.

'What?' Zak said sharply.

'Glandular fever,' Matt repeated.

There was a moment of silence.

'Shucks!' said Zak. 'I take it all back.'

'You mean I've finally said something right?' asked Carole.

Matt smiled, picked up a fragment of mortar from the floor and aimlessly threw it. It should have landed at Carole's feet but the shimmering air absorbed it, absorbed the throat lozenge Carole aimed at him. He smiled again at her effort. It was a barrier, he said, which nothing could pass through and it was not just space between them but time as well. He glanced at his wristwatch. One hundred and thirty five years, six months, two days and fourteen hours to be precise, he said. In his time it was July 23rd 2121.

Carole gaped at him. Even when Matt explained it was not imaginable. She could not envisage a hundred and thirty-five years into the future. England was ruled from Brussels, he told her. Energy came from the sun and there was no nuclear power, no major world problems

32

and not much political dissension. And the latest American space ship was about to take off for the stars. There was not a soul left alive who remembered when Carole lived. The twentieth century was ancient history and Gossington Square was derelict and due to be demolished.

'That's why we're here,' said Matt. 'There aren't many old houses left. This is the only one in the area which is empty and reputed to be haunted. It's not exactly safe but we had to take the chance. A couple of weeks from now the house will be flattened and its ghosts will be gone.'

'Are you saying you're a ghost-buster?' Carole asked him.

'That's right,' said Matt. 'And you're busted. We were hoping for the housemaid who committed suicide but we'll settle for you.'

'I'm not a ghost!' Carole said indignantly.

'Aren't you?' Matt said quietly.

Her insides lurched. His smile was sad and he was looking at her gently, tenderly, not wanting to distress her but wanting her to understand . . . from where he stood, one hundred and thirty-five years in the future, Carole was dead. She thought she must have died without knowing it, that very morning, before she had even lived. She wanted to scream and deny it, tell him he was wrong, that she was still alive and would go on living, but then Mrs Dawkins came into the room.

'How are you feeling, my dear?'

Carole froze, looked towards Matt, but it seemed Mrs Dawkins did not see him. She simply walked through the curtain of shimmering air and picked up the throat lozenge that lay on the carpet . . . and as she did so, everything vanished. The room was as it had been before, wintry and cold, with snow fluttering against the window pane and the clock on the mantelpiece saying ten past one.

*

Carole was dead, Matt had said, but she did not tell her mother. Even to her own mind it seemed crazy. Yet she needed to convince herself she was alive. She noticed the heat in the bathroom and the scent of talc, the taste of kedgeree her mother cooked for supper. And that night she lay awake feeling the blankets rough and warm to her touch, remembering the television serial she had sat and watched, hearing the tick of the clock, the rattle of the window and the whine of the wind in the chimney breast. All those things assured her she was alive. Unless they were illusions? Maybe, she thought, life was a dream and when she awoke she would find herself dead? Or maybe Matt had been an omen? A cold moon shone on the snow in Gossington Squre and she was afraid to sleep, afraid to let go of her awareness of herself and the world. And in the morning, when her mother drew back the curtains, Carole was pale and tired and dark shadows ringed her eyes. She looked like death warmed up, her mother said.

'Maybe it's terminal,' Carole said agitatedly.

'What?' enquired her mother.

'Glandular fever.'

'That's highly unlikely,' her mother replied.

It was a kind of reassurance and Carole's own common sense told her that ghosts didn't need to eat breakfast or write school essays, did not stub their toes on the table leg or suffer from headaches and swollen glands. They did not fancy other ghosts either, but Carole spent the morning waiting and hoping Matt would return, materialize from the thin air of her room . . . a ghost from the future as she was a ghost from the past. Nothing happened. Her eyes grew leaden and heat shimmered above the convector fire . . . and Mrs Dawkins woke her at one o'clock with chicken soup for lunch.

Had it not been for Splodge Carole might have believed she had invented the whole incident. But that cat was behaving very peculiarly, Mrs Dawkins said. He had spent yesterday afternoon and evening crouching behind the sofa and refusing to come out. And earlier that morning, when Mrs Dawkins had picked him up intending to bring him upstairs for Carole, he had sworn and struggled like a wildcat and finally scratched her, fled downstairs to the basement boiler room and escaped through the partly open window.

'I can't think what's come over him,' Mrs Dawkins said worriedly.

Carole knew. A couple of ghost-busters from A D 2121 had scared Splodge half to death. And all afternoon she heard Mrs Dawkins calling across the back gardens. It made her feel guilty thinking of Splodge out in the cold snow, cowering among the cabbages and afraid to come home, while she sat by the convector heater wanting nothing more than for Matt and Zak to reappear and feeling disappointed they did not.

Cats had short memories. Splodge returned the following morning, but as the days went by Carole's disappointment turned to depression. The snow melted and snowdrops bloomed beneath the lime trees in the Square and Matt's absence haunted her. She thought she would not have minded if he *had* proved her to be a ghost because her life, as it was, was hardly worth living. She was sick of having glandular fever, sick of being confined to the house, fed up with everything.

'I might as well be dead!' she announced.

Her mother was marking school exercise books.

'Why's that?' she said.

'Well, what's there to live for?' Carole asked.

'There's next week's episode of *Dallas*.'

'Who cares about *Dallas*?'

'Tomorrow's dinner then?'

'I'm being serious,' Carole said cuttingly.

'So am I,' her mother replied. 'What else do we live for but the little mundane things of life? If we sit around waiting for the few rare, wonderful moments that make it all worthwhile we may as well not live at all.'

'That's what I meant!' said Carole.

'You'll get over it,' her mother promised.

Splodge got over it. Accompanied by Mrs Dawkins he made a few nervous forays into Carole's room and, finding nothing to alarm him, took up residency again on the candlewick counterpane. He was better than no one, Carole supposed. And when February began with two days of freezing rain she followed Splodge's example, sighed and forgot . . . until she awoke that night and saw beyond the wall of shimmering air the room full of sunset light and Matt standing there. It was four in the morning according to the clock on the mantelpiece, and Carole did not know if she were glad or furious, or how to react.

'Where have you been?' she hissed.

'Checking,' he told her.

'Where's Zak?'

'He's checking too . . . at the Central Records Office.'

Carole draped her dressing gown around her shoulders.

'So how long does it take?' she asked him. 'You've been checking for ten days already and all I gave you was my name and address!'

Matt looked surprised. The sunset was brassy behind him and trees drooped in the summer heat. Owls hooted in the derelict Square. When Mrs Dawkins had entered the room the time circuit had snapped, he explained. He had tried to get back to her as quickly as possible but obviously the passage of time in past and future was not the same. Carole's ten days was his yesterday and his early evening was the middle of her night.

'I'm sorry,' he said honestly.

She was glad anyway, glad he was back, but with her mother sleeping in the next bedroom their conversation had to be in whispers. He needed to talk to her, he said, alone, before Zak returned from the Central Records

36

Office. Something had been worrying him, nagging at his mind ever since Carole had first appeared. It was not just the fact that he could see and hear her and Zak could not, nor was it the fact that the machines failed to register her presence . . . it was the fact that her behaviour was inconsistent with any known psychic phenomenon. In other words she did not act like a ghost.

'Nor do you,' Carole told him.

'Well, I'm not a ghost,' he said.

'Yes, you are,' said Carole. 'You don't have any substance and I can see straight through you, so what else can you be? And if I'm dead to you then you're dead to me . . . or rather, you're not yet born. I mean, why should I have to prove I'm real when you're not real either?'

Matt stared at her.

'I don't understand,' he said.

'Now you know how I feel,' Carole told him.

Matt ran a hand through his blond unruly curls. He was as confused as she had been for the last ten days, her mind going around in circles trying to work it out. Now it was his turn to think himself a ghost. She could see the stones of the wall through the cat-suit he was wearing, the broken window through his eyes. They were blue, she thought, bright as a midday sky. But the impression faded among leaves of trees and the roseate hues of sunset. She was a ghost seeing a ghost and was tempted to laugh, but maybe it was not so funny. Surrounded by midwinter darkness and all the trappings of her own reality, Carole ached with the sheer impossibility of knowing him.

'What *is* this?' he asked her.

'I don't know,' she replied.

'I'm alive, so I can't be a ghost.'

'In that case I'm not one either because I'm alive too.'

'That's impossible.'

'But it's true,' said Carole.

'Zak's never going to believe it.'

'But you do?' Carole asked anxiously.

'I suppose that's why I wanted to talk to you,' he said.

'So what do we do now?'

'Prove it?' he sighed.

Carole approached the veil of shimmering air. Matt was beyond it, so close that she thought she could touch him if she reached out her hand. Maybe he read her mind and knew her feelings, wanted her to be real just as she wanted him. Or maybe they did not think at all. Time had no meaning until Carole stepped into it and found herself alone. The room was dark. Rain lashed the window glass. Matt and the summer world and the hoot of owls were gone.

Several days passed before Matt reappeared. Carole was sitting in the armchair beside the convector heater writing an essay on the French Revolution, when she heard the hum of the time displacement machine. She held her breath as the shimmering air dissolved the walls and window and the morning faded to a future midnight. Both Matt and Zak were there but she had no chance to speak to them for Splodge, asleep on the bed, suddenly awoke and was aware. He seemed to go berserk, a madcat spitting and swearing and trying to escape. Ears flattened, tail fluffed and belly touching the floor, he headed for the door, found it shut and fled beneath the bed, emerged on the other side and shot through the time barrier before Carole could stop him. Claws raked the velvet curtains. Jigsaws and the Monopoly set, stored on top of the wardrobe, fell as he leapt. And there he stayed, cowering behind a wicker basket full of dolls' clothes, peering down with green eyes bigger than gobstoppers and a slightly puzzled expression on his splodgy black and white face. He had broken the circuit. The room was as it should be. February sunlight lay bright on the pink patterned carpet and only Carole was mad.

'You great stupid idiot!' she yelled.

She left the door open, spent the rest of the day sorting out thousands of jigsaw pieces, and what should have been a beautiful encounter had been ended before it began. Then her fever, which had abated, returned worse than ever. Her head throbbed, and Paracetamols ceased to have any effect, and even in bed she had to wear a woollen scarf tied tight around her neck to ease the pain. Her mother filled hot-water bottles before she left for school and each morning, on her way to the Oxfam shop, Mrs Dawkins looked in and made her a honey-and-lemon drink. Freezing mist hung outside the window, made ghostly the lime trees that grew in the Square and isolated Carole from the world. Not that she cared. Snuggled in bed with the cat she felt miserable enough to want to be left alone and she was not particularly pleased when the room started buzzing and shimmering, Splodge had another nervous breakdown in his hurry to escape, and Matt and Zak re-established their connections.

'Carole?' said Matt.

Clouds hid the moon and a flashlight shone on crumbling walls, touched the bright elusive blue of his eyes. DON'T BUG ME, the slogan on Zak's T-shirt said. Their voices seemed to come from far away, from a future England in the grip of a heatwave. And how could it be only an hour since Splodge broke the circuit? Only yesterday that Carole had last talked with Matt. Days and weeks were muddled in her head but it was some consolation to learn that she was not about to die of glandular fever. Zak had traced her birth certificate, Matt informed her, but had found no record of her death. Presumably she was going to live and marry and change her name, but as twentieth-century records were not computerized he could not tell her who her future husband would be. Having met Matt Carole was not really interested anyway, and nor was Zak. Her future was beside the point, he said. And finding her birth certificate might prove she had existed once, but it did not prove she existed now, either as a living person or a ghost.

'If she's real we need evidence!' said Zak.

'We could try some awareness tests,' suggested Matt.

'Right now I don't feel like it,' Carole said.

'Yes,' said Matt. 'Something like that. You feel, therefore you are, and that makes two of us. But I'm not sure about Zak.'

Now and then, Carole could never tell when, but throughout their hot July nights where buff moths fluttered and her February mornings of frost and sun and rain, she tried to convince Zak she was a thinking, feeling, living human being. Her breath made mist on the cold surface of a mirror. She bled when she was scratched, burned when she touched a naked flame. She could deduce, debate, argue, agree or disagree, laugh, cry, hate and love. Yet she could prove nothing because Matt was her only witness and he could be making her up. Not even when she read a passage from a daily paper which checked out verbatim, was Zak convinced. It could be some weird telepathic link-up, he said, Matt's mind picking up vibes from the past.

'What does it take?' Carole asked despairingly.

'After five hundred repeat performances he might be swayed,' said Matt. 'You know what they say about scientists? If they can't dissect something or examine it under a microscope then it doesn't exist. At least you have God for company.'

'And you,' Carole said softly.

'I'm beginning to wish,' he replied.

'If we were really ghosts . . .'

'Don't,' he said gently.

'If there were just some way . . .'

'There isn't.'

But maybe there was, Carole thought afterwards. Flies caught in amber survived through geological aeons and time capsules were sent into space, or buried under concrete for future generations to find. There had to be something Carole could give that would survive a mere one hundred and thirty-five years, something that would reach Matt and prove to Zak she were real. All night Carole thought of it, eager for morning and needing to act. And it was nothing to do with glandular fever that her eyes shone and her cheeks were flushed. She actually felt better, she told her mother.

Later, when the house was empty and Mrs Dawkins had gone with the shopping trolley to collect the weekly groceries, Carole wrote Matt a letter. She enclosed it with a photograph, a lock of her hair and a blackcurrant throat lozenge, inside the silver box. At home he had one like it, he had said, but this box was Carole's. It was engraved with vine leaves and cherubs and had been given to her by her grandmother before she died. Carefully Carole wrapped it in newspaper and sealed it in a polythene bag. Then she fetched tools from the kitchen, prized away the boarding and placed the package on a ledge in the chimney. Her hands were black with soot and she had to hammer the bent nails straight before she could fix the board back into position. Exertion made her feel ill again but she knew it would be worth it, worth everything to prove herself alive.

February gave way to March. Crocuses bloomed, yellow and purple beneath the lime trees in the Square, and sparrows nested. If the weather was fine, the doctor said, it might do Carole some good to go outside for a breath of fresh air. But she staged a relapse, fearing Matt might appear when she were gone. And the next morning her relapse was genuine. Her head ached, her temperature was up, and the glands in her neck pained

41

something awful. And, spooked once too often, Splodge
refused to keep her company, clawed his way from Mrs
Dawkins' arms and fled. She spent the day in bed and
alone, wondering all over again if she would ever
recover.

'Of course you will,' her mother said positively.

'Maybe I don't want to,' Carole said dramatically.
'Maybe I'd rather die and fall in love with a ghost.'

Her mother laughed.

'Love is a symptom of life,' she said. 'But the dead are
dead and don't have feelings.'

And that was proof, thought Carole. When Matt read
her letter he would know for sure she was alive. Each
new day dawned with a kind of nervous anticipation, an
experience of relief when her mother went to school and
Mrs Dawkins left for the Oxfam shop, a morning of
waiting and hoping, another disappointment. Then
someone moved into the upstairs flat. A music student
with long hair, Mrs Dawkins said disapprovingly. And
Carole had something else to contend with. She listened
to his footsteps walking the floors overhead, the sound
of his radio, the flush of water and the slam of his door.
She heard him practising endless scales on a clarinet. He
was not intrusive exactly, not over-loud and inconsider-
ate, yet he was there and she was constantly aware of
him. She felt inhibited and no longer free, afraid that
when Matt came back she might be overheard and her
secret discovered. She wanted the house to herself
again, hoped the ghost of the housemaid would drive
him away but, to the plaintive notes of a clarinet con-
certo, it finally happened.

The still air shimmered and wet grey daylight beyond the
window slowly darkened to a July night. Carole forgot
about the student. There was a thrill inside her and her
heart beat faster, and the music was gone in a rumble of
thunder and a deluge of summer rain. White with plaster

dust and opaque as milk, it dripped through the ceiling and splattered on to the floor, and behind Matt's eyes she saw the lightning flicker, saw the flash of his smile.

'How are you, Carole?'

'Better,' she breathed.

But Zak was in no mood for preliminaries. He was worried about the effects of the lightning on his time displacement machine, about safety factors and the roof falling in and the fact he was getting wet. Tape recorder at the ready, Zak simply wanted to collect the routine data and return to campus. Never mind how Carole was feeling, he said. All Matt needed to ask was the time and date, what the weather was doing and the main newspaper headlines which they could check with the met office and archives in the morning . . . then they could both go home.

'Because I'm not hanging around here all night while you chat up the wall,' Zak concluded.

'No one asked you to,' Matt informed him.

'So why don't you stick to the business in hand?'

'Why don't you push off right now?' Matt suggested.

'And leave you in charge of my equipment?' said Zak. 'No way, buddy! Besides, I might miss something.'

Matt sighed, turned to Carole.

'That's the trouble with gooseberries,' he said. 'They're too thick-skinned to understand.'

Carole laughed.

'He will in a minute,' she promised.

'I doubt it,' said Matt.

But Carole had written Matt a letter. It would prove she was real, she said, that she had been aware of him and Zak from the moment she had met them. She had written it down, everything that had happened, all her perceptions and all her feelings. She had put it on a ledge up the chimney, in the silver box. And maybe it was not exactly scientific but it was the only thing she could think of which was part of herself, the only thing she could give Matt which was likely to survive . . . a letter, a lock of her hair and a blackcurrant throat lozenge.

'What's she say?' asked Zak impatiently.

'She says . . .'

Matt shook his head, grinned, then laughed in delight. His eyes shone blue in the torch light. 'You're beautiful,' he told Carole, and turned away.

'So what's she say?' Zak repeated.

'Wait and I'll show you,' said Matt.

Lightning flashed on the fairness of his hair, and the ceiling dripped and bulged as he approached the chimney breast. There the darkness absorbed him. Carole heard the rotting wood give way as he tore at the boarding, heard Zak's warning cry. She hardly knew what happened next. There was a noise like thunder and her scream mixed with Zak's as the roof beam fell and Matt was buried under tons of rubble. Then there was only Zak, tearing at the stones and plaster chunks and trying to free him, a ghost in the torchlight unashamedly weeping, knowing, when he found him, Matt would be injured or dead.

Carole wept too, loudly and hysterically, not caring that the door opened or who came into the room. He wore blue denim jeans and all she could do was scream at him . . . 'Help him! Help him!' . . . watch as he walked towards the shimmering curtain of air and Zak dragged out the body. 'Dead!' sobbed Zak. 'Oh, no . . . not you, Matt!' Then it was over, ended, everything gone. The circuit was broken and Carole was left in the wet grey morning, heart-broken and wretched, with a total stranger.

He spread his hands.

'There was nothing I could do,' he said sadly.

'No,' choked Carole.

'And you don't need to be upset. They were only ghosts and that's how ghosts behave. They relive the moments of their deaths over and over. I've got one upstairs. She walks around my bedroom with a carving knife and there's nothing I can do for her either.'

'You don't understand,' sobbed Carole.

'No one can change the past,' he said gently.

'But Matt lived in the future!' wept Carole. 'And it's my fault he's dead. I didn't need to prove I was real because he knew anyway. If I hadn't put that box up the chimney . . .'

The student was kind and quiet, lending her his handkerchief, making her sit in the kitchen and making her coffee, listening as she talked. He did not say she was crazy or imagining things, or that he himself would have to be mad to believe her. He did not say anything, just listened and waited until she was done. Rain in the ensuing silence fell softly on the roof of the outhouse and the window steamed as Carole wiped her eyes for the thousandth time and finally looked at him. He was staring thoughtfully at the dregs in his coffee cup . . . a young man with fair shoulder-length hair and bright blue eyes. For some reason he reminded her of Matt and once more the silly tears began to flow.

'What'll I do?' she whimpered. 'How can I live with it, knowing that I caused his death? How can I bear it?'

He pushed back his chair.

'Maybe you won't have to,' he said. 'It hasn't happened yet, has it? Not for Matt. For him it won't happen for another hundred and thirty-five years. We can't change the past but we can change the future. Do you have a screwdriver or something?'

Uncomprehendingly Carole dragged her mother's tool box from the broom cupboard, watched him select a claw hammer and disappear into the bedroom. The nails gave way easily and he prized away the board that sealed the chimney, returned a minute later with the silver box in his hand. If Carole got rid of it, he said, then Matt would have no reason to go to the chimney breast, no reason to be standing there when the ceiling fell. He would not die and she would not be responsible. And was it really as simple as that?

She watched him open the pedal bin.

'Yes?' he asked.

Carole hesitated. The box was an heirloom. It was old and valuable and somehow it seemed wrong to throw it away. Yet she did not want to keep it. It bound her to Matt and her own memories, to the distant future when he would be living and she would be dead. She supposed she could sell it to an antique shop but that seemed wrong too.

'Yes?' the student repeated.

'No,' said Carole.

She took it from him, tipped the contents in the bin, then handed it back.

'You keep it,' she said.

He frowned.

'Are you sure?'

'Please,' she said earnestly. 'I'd like you to have it.'

He smiled then, and his smile was like Matt's. He would treasure it, he promised, use it as a paper weight and think of her. Dull silver it shone in his hand and she felt it belonged with him, that by giving it to him she had not parted with it at all, or parted with Matt. She had the peculiar feeling that nothing had changed because nothing had happened and the future began in his eyes. She was glad she had met him, grateful for all he had done, for his blond hair and his bright blue eyes and the squeeze of her arm when he turned to go. But Splodge, washing his backside on the landing carpet, took one look at him and fled.

'What's up with the cat?' he asked.

'He thinks he's seen a ghost,' said Carole.

And in a way Splodge had.

'My name, by the way, is John Boyd-Hamilton with a hyphen,' the student said. 'Fancy coming for a pizza on Saturday night?'

Buzz-Words

JAN MARK

'Why shouldn't bees have souls?' Maurice said.

'What do they want souls for?' Nina asked. 'They don't go to church.'

'There was that wasps' nest over the altar at St Anselm's Without.'

'They weren't there to worship,' Nazzer said. 'They didn't know it was a silly place to park until the men from the council moved in.'

'Well, you get these nutters that think animals go to heaven. They have pet cemeteries with little crosses: *In Memory of Dear Rover. United with Gran.*'

'The nutters who worry me are the ones who think *they're* going to heaven.'

'What about worms? There aren't going to be worms in heaven. What about tsetse flies?'

'Worms don't have souls,' Nazzer said. 'They don't even have brains. They have ganglia. If you mince up an educated worm and feed it to an ignorant one, the ignorant worm gets clever.'

'How do you test a worm's IQ?' Nina said. 'My sister had a ganglion, on the side of her little toe. She hit it with a book and it disappeared. That's standard practice for ganglions.'

'You get much the same effect with worms, I dare say,' Nazzer remarked, 'if you hit them with a book.'

'They'll have to keep the numbers down somehow.'

'Where?'

'In heaven. There's more insects in one English garden than there are Chinese.'

'There's no Chinese in our garden,' Nina said. 'Anyway, there's no point in animals having souls. They don't have a sense of sin.'

'Dogs have a sense of sin,' Maurice said.

'They have a sense of guilt,' Nazzer said. 'Most of them look guilty all the time, even when they haven't done anything, except for those mongrels that grin and run sideways.'

'OK,' Nina said, 'there'll be dogs in heaven, but they've got to draw the line somewhere. They'll have a sort of interviewing room, like down the social security, with a counter, and St Peter asking test questions, you know: "Well, Tiddles, are you sorry you ate the budgie?" '

'That wouldn't work,' Nazzer said. 'Tiddles will say, "No, I am not sorry I ate the budgie because that is what budgies are for and anyway, I already got booted for eating the budgie, also for making a nest in the shredded wheat. You're not going to send me down for that, are you, Guv?" '

'Tiddles will go to Limbo,' Maurice said. 'A sort of Butlins for cats and atheists.'

'I think it'll be like Customs,' Nina said. 'People with nothing on their consciences will go through the green channel, like Tiddles and his budgie—nothing to declare.'

'What about the budgie?' Nazzer said. 'Where's that going?'

'That wouldn't work either,' Maurice said. 'Think of all the villains and loonies with nothing on their consciences. Hitler would go through the green channel.'

'They'll be on the lookout for Hitler,' Nazzer said. 'They'll have something more foolproof than the green channel.'

'Well, they've got God, haven't they? He'll do the real sorting out.'

'God delegates,' Maurice said. 'That's what he's good at. Don't forget the middle management.'

'Clergymen?'

'I was thinking of angels.'

'Angels sit on the Board and have executive lunches. They make policy decisions. Bishops are more area supervisors.'

'That's only for people; there's got to be someone looking out for the non-human clients. You know, East Midlands Superintendent of Dogs, Goats and Large Rodents.'

'What about the bees?'

'The bees are going to Butlins, aren't they? With the atheists.'

'I think you've got it wrong about atheists. It's pagans who get off with a caution. I should think atheists will be interned.'

'Like I said, Butlins. Atheists won't be expecting heaven, anyway, will they? They'll just expect to be dead.'

'Bees won't be expecting heaven, either,' Nina said. 'I mean, that's what we were saying, isn't it? They just spend their lives being bees. They don't try to be *better* bees.'

'That's the trouble with evolution,' Nazzer said. 'There's no incentive to try harder, no productivity bonus. Natural selection does it for you.'

'What about reincarnation?' Maurice said. 'That's an incentive, if you like. If you don't do well enough the first time round you come back as a bee.'

'That would solve the overcrowding problem,' Nina said. 'All the atheists will have to start over as bees and work up through rats and goats until they get human status again. That way you just end up with people.'

'Not necessarily,' Maurice said. 'For all we know bees

are at the top of the list. We may be bad bees, working our way up to being bees again. People may be the bottom rung of the ladder. Bees may turn out to be the highest form of life, soul-wise.'

'If they've got souls.'

'I mean, they do better than most people, most of the time, don't they? Well organized, stable economy—'

'One party politics.'

'And moral. They're much more moral than we are. They sting each other to death.'

'Your average bee,' Nazzer said, 'is not particularly intelligent.'

'I never said it was. I said bees are well organized.'

'Someone's got to do the organizing,' Nina said. 'Stands to reason, there's got to be one intelligent bee calling the shots.'

'Bees have a corporate mentality,' Maurice said.

'Like Japanese office workers,' Nina said. 'They all stand up in the morning and sing the Company song.'

'I suppose it's a kind of collective subconscious, isn't it?' Maurice said. 'No one gives the orders, they just know what to do instinctively, so they do it.'

'Programmed,' Nina said. 'I mean, don't you need a brain, for instinct? Bees don't have brains, do they, Naz? Any more than worms.'

'I don't think anyone's ever run an encephalograph on a bee,' Nazzer said.

'They must have some sort of a brain,' Maurice said. 'Even fleas have brains, they must have. How else do they learn to do tricks? Bees are bigger than fleas.'

'Bison are bigger than people,' Nazzer observed. 'Come to that, bison are bigger than fleas. A bison-sized flea could do a lot of damage; a kind of intercontinental ballistic bison. How far would it be able to jump, Maurice.'

'Wouldn't work,' Maurice said. 'The skeleton would collapse under the weight.'

'Fleas are exoskeletal,' Nazzer said. 'It's a different principle entirely.'

'It doesn't make any difference whether you wear your bones on the outside or the inside,' Maurice said. 'They still have to carry your weight. Gravity's always a problem. If you dropped a flea down a deep hole it wouldn't notice. A bison would burst.'

'What about cats, then?' Nina said. 'Cats are smaller than dogs, but they're a sight brighter. You never get a cat letting anyone teach it tricks. Ever seen a performing cat?'

'It's got nothing to do with the size,' Maurice said. 'It's brain area. Better to have a small wrinkled surface than a large smooth one.'

'You should know,' Nina said.

'Walnuts are more intelligent than almonds,' Nazzer said; 'it's a well known fact.'

'It still wouldn't mean they've got souls.'

'Walnuts?'

'Bees.'

'There was a film once: *The Spirit of the Hive*.'

'That was foreign.'

'They've got ghosts,' Maurice said.

'Phantom bees?'

'No, that's what I meant by corporate mentality; not individual bees, a whole swarm.'

'Why not phantom bats?' Nina said, meaningly, 'in the belfry?'

'I don't know about bats,' Maurice said, 'but look at that.'

'Your arm? I've seen that before, somewhere,' Nina said.

'And what's that on my arm?'

'Hairs,' Nazzer said. 'And a pimple. And that scar where Jaggers tried to saw you in half with a ruler. Are you going to put it on exhibition. I'll write you a guide book if you cut me in on the takings.'

'Drop the wisecracks,' Maurice said. 'What are *these*?'

'Flea bites,' Nina said. 'Who've you been snogging with, Anna Witchard? Don't you know about the Witchards?'

'That's nits,' Nazzer said. 'All the nits in North Norfolk come from the Witchards. Every time they move there's a new outbreak.'

'These are not nit bites, they're bee stings,' Maurice said. 'And look here, on my neck.'

'Never knew Anna Witchard had such sharp teeth.'

'Nits.'

'Don't you know a bee sting when you see one? There's two more on my back, lower down.'

'I don't think we want to see them, thanks all the same,' Nina said.

'Bee stings in February?' Nazzer said. 'Pull the other one.'

'If I had nits I wouldn't advertise them in the canteen,' Nina said.

'It'll be a special species of winter bee,' Nazzer said, 'imported from the Soviet Union. They have extra long fur and leather wings. There used to be quite a trade in beeskin coats until the Hymenoptera Liberation Front moved in.'

'Get lost,' Maurice said. 'These were the usual sort of bee, only they died last week and they stung me on Saturday.'

'Like my grandad,' Nina said. 'Gran last saw him six months after he died.'

'Did he sting her?' Nazzer said.

'No, he was standing on the bend in the stairs. It was during a power cut and she was just going up to bed with a candle when she saw him there. She said afterwards that she didn't think much about it at first because he always did spend a lot of time just standing about, and then she remembered he was dead, so she went back down again for another look. He was still there. He said,

"Hello, Edith," and she said, "Hello, Arnold," and he said, "I've just come back to see how you're getting on," and she said, "I'm all right, thank you, Arnold," and he said, "Well, I'll be going, then," and he stood around for a bit longer and then he sort of went frilly at the edges and disappeared. Mum was furious with her when she told us. She thought Gran ought to have asked him where he'd come back *from* and what it was like. Gran said, "Well, he never did have much to say for himself, did he?" '

'I expect she imagined it,' Nazzer said. 'Like you said, she was used to seeing him standing around.'

'Yes, but she said it was exactly like him.'

'Of course it was. That's *just* how she would have imagined him. If this goat, say, had turned up on the stairs with horns and yellow eyes and said, "Hello, I am Arnold, back from the grave," that *would* have been convincing.'

'Did she have any proof?' Maurice said.

'What sort of proof?'

'Supernatural marks; like my bee stings?'

'Supernatural nits.'

'Look, forget the nits. These are bee stings and I got them on Saturday when I went over to Hickling.'

'I meant to ask you about that,' Nina said. 'You were supposed to be helping with the coffee morning.'

'I rang up,' Maurice said. 'I rang twice, but there was no one in. Where were you?'

'*I* was at the coffee morning,' Nina said.

'I was digging out tree stumps, in this weather, I ask you. You know what it was like on Saturday,' Maurice said. 'I went out expecting pneumonia and what do I get? Bee stings.'

'So you keep saying. I think this is just a cover-up for some horrible disease you've got and there's no known cure,' Nazzer said. 'They're buboes.'

'They are not buboes. Listen, you know my uncle does

landscape gardening? Well, he had this big job on over the weekend and his partner was off sick—'

'Told you,' Nazzer said. 'I suppose he'd come out in lumps, too.'

'Yes, he had. Look, if you'll just listen; my Uncle Dave rang up on Friday night and said that Joe—that's his partner—had been taken ill at work and could I come over and help? Well, I didn't know what had happened, neither did he, so I said I'd go.

'I hitched a lift over to Hickling—*after* I'd tried to ring you, Nina, and there's Dave in the kitchen with Joe's wife, and she's carrying on about Joe being delirious and covered in stings. Only we didn't know about it being stings, then, and she always does go over the top. Every little earache's meningitis. She said he'd come home from work all swelled up and moaning about buzzing in his head, but he couldn't see anything. I thought she meant that his eyes were so swelled he couldn't see anything.'

'They do a lot of swelling up over that way, don't they,' Nina said. 'I don't know that I go for all this with the stings. It could be some sort of lurgy that no one knows anything about.'

'Like I said,' Nazzer muttered, 'a plague, unknown to science. Millions will perish.'

'Only if they go to Hickling first,' Maurice said. 'Dave was worried in case it was some sort of pesticide and Joe was reacting to it. *They* never use it; he's very organic, Dave is; chews his compost up with his own teeth, sort of thing, but you never know what people have been putting on the land, out there. Anyway, Joe's wife swore he'd been stung and the doctor said that's what it looked like, so we got in the Land Rover and went over to see.'

'The swellings?'

'No, the site; Tokesby Holmes Farm. You know how much rain there's been lately; it looked like the Battle of the Somme. The house was behind some bushes—it's a bungalow, actually; you can only see the telly aerial over the top of the hedge—and there was a sort of shed. Everything else was mud and trenches. The sky was grey and it was drizzling. There was thick orange water in the trenches and this big dip in the middle, like a shell crater. Any minute you expected someone to open up with a mortar or some guy in a tin hat leap over an embankment and whop you with an entrenching tool. I mean, remember when we went to the Imperial War Museum and they had those mock-ups of trench warfare?'

'Yeah,' Nina said, 'those spiked gloves and things. It looked more like the Middle Ages than seventy years ago.'

'Those mock-ups were dead cosy compared to Tokesby Holmes. You know, we were standing there, and the Land Rover was up to its axles, and I suddenly realized what it must have been like. I mean, you could feel yourself *rotting*. There wasn't any grass, nothing green at all, just mud and tree stumps. Every now and again something went plop, like gas coming out of a swamp. I never saw anything like it. Usually when Dave does a landscape it's turf and rhododendrons and *Cupressus Leylandii*.'

'What's *Cupressus Leylandii*?' Nina asked.

'BL Tree Division,' Nazzer said.

'I said, "What have you been up to, Dave?" and he says, "It's not us, do us a favour, it's those silly sods up at the farm." Well, you know what it's like round here, they've got a thing about trees. I think it's a primitive race memory left over from the time when we were all plants.'

'Speak for yourself,' Nina said. 'Personally, I've never been a plant.'

'I meant the Common Ancestor.'

'I thought the Common Ancestor was some kind of orang-utan,' Nazzer said.

'It could just as easily have been a tree. I think it's deep-seated envy. As soon as any tree gets over six feet tall they cut it down. They don't even like hedges, much. If a hedge looks like it's doing too well for itself, they grub it up and put in ranch fencing or breeze blocks; something that won't grow. Dave said, "They didn't leave it to us to clear the land, they did it themselves. Bloody townies." Then I realized it wasn't a farm at all, just a house on some land that *had* been a farm. Typical. The last trees in the area and they go and cut them down. Only they hadn't just chopped them down, they'd started digging the roots out and then found they couldn't manage it so they'd got Dave and Joe in to finish the job. The trees that were down were little ones—I think it had been a coppice. The one we had to deal with was an oak; well, it had been an oak. There was only the roots left and about four feet of trunk—and a pile of ash. So we sort of swam over to have a look.

' "We'll need a tractor and chains for this," Dave says and then another voice says, "I said they shouldn't do it."

'I never jumped so high in my life. One moment there was just us and the mud, and then out of nowhere, this voice. So we looked up and there was this little kid, about ten, standing on the bank in the rain, wearing an oilskin and sou'wester and boots. You could tell he wasn't local, the local kids wear camouflage gear and balaclava helmets, like the IRA. This one looked more like Christopher Robin.'

'Your sister's boy?'

'No, Christopher Robin from *Winnie the Pooh*. You know, with Eeyore and Piglet.'

'Funny friends, you've got,' Nazzer said.

'It's a *book*,' Nina said. 'They all lived in a tree and pretended to be clouds.'

'Funny reading habits you've got.'

'Well, he just stood there, looking at us, and Dave said, "Come again?" and this little kid says, "I told them not to do it."

' "What's your name, then?" Dave says, and the little

kid says, "Sebastian," and Dave says, "Well, you come down here, Sebastian. You make me nervous up there. That bank's going to give way at any moment." So Sebastian came down. He jumped. There was this puddle in the crater right next to us and he jumped into it. Dave said, "I asked for that," so I just wiped the mud off my tonsils and didn't kill anyone.

'Sebastian says, "That was my camp."

' "Played soldiers, did you?" Dave says. "With your mates?"

' "I haven't got any mates," Sebastian says. He didn't sound sad, he was just telling us. "My mates are at St Radigund's. I don't know anybody here."

' "Where's St Radigund's?" Dave says.

' "Near Canterbury," says Sebastian. Then I realized he must go away to school. I felt really sorry for him, I can tell you. All his friends at the other end of the country and him stuck there for weeks on end in No Man's Land.

' "Are you on half term, then?" I said, and he nodded. *Then* he started looking sad. "I came back on Friday night," he said. "It was all dark, so I didn't come out here till this morning. Mummy said what they'd done but I didn't know what it would look like."

'Dave looked interested. He said, "Do you know what happened to Joe?"

'Sebastian said, "Who's Joe?"

'Dave said, "He's my partner. He was here yesterday."

'Sebastian gave us a very funny look. He said, "Did you do all this? You and Joe?"

'I think Dave caught on then, that while Sebastian was away at St Radigund's, getting educated, his loving parents had moved in with a chain saw and flattened his camp. "No," he says, very quickly, "we didn't do any of it. Mr Phillips—he your dad?"

' "Yes," says Sebastian, the way you might say, "Yes, I've got diphtheria."

' "Your dad started clearing this hollow to make an alpine garden," says Dave, though it looked more like an alpine bog to me, "only he's having a bit of trouble shifting the tree roots, so he called us in. We're landscape gardeners."

' "What's a landscape gardener?" says the lad.

' "Well, we do gardens on a big scale," says Dave. "We're used to moving earth and tree roots; we've got the equipment. We'd probably have made a better job of it than your old dad." He couldn't resist saying that, I could see.

'Sebastian says, "What happened to Joe?" and he had that funny look again, like he had a very good idea what had happened to Joe.

'Dave said, "He had a bit of an accident. He came over here yesterday afternoon to see what needed doing. Your dad was going to show him round the potholes, like."

' "What sort of an accident?" says Sebastian.

' "Well, we don't rightly know," says Dave. "He looks like he's been stung quite badly. We wondered whether your dad had been using pesticides."

' "What's pesticides?" says Sebastian. *Definitely* not local. I don't know what they teach them at St Radigund's.

' "Poisons," I said. "Poisons for insects."

' "Oh, yes," says the lad. "Daddy used some poison last week. And he got stung, too. Yesterday. When Mummy and me came back last night he was in bed, all swollen up."

'And he laughed. I didn't think it was very nice, laughing because your dad's all swollen up, but then I remembered what Sebastian's dad had done to his camp.

'Dave was getting a bit worried by now. He says, "Does your dad know what stung him?" and Sebastian says, "No, but I do," and then he says again, "I told him he shouldn't do it."

'Dave got very serious. He squats down in the mud in front of the lad and he says, "Look, son, this could be dangerous. What do you know?"

'Sebastian didn't say anything for a bit. He just stood there, we all stood there, in the rain. It was coming on harder, running down our faces, only Sebastian was under his sou'wester. It wasn't rain running down *his* face. Then he said, "It was *my* camp. It was *my* tree. It was *my* bees."

'Dave says, "Bees? At this time of year?"

'Sebastian says, "They go to sleep in winter. He didn't dare do it in the summer. They were *savage* bees."

'Dave looked at me. He looked at Sebastian. He says, "There's no sense in us getting soaked, come and sit in the cab."

'We went back to the Land Rover, with Sebastian sitting between us. He took his sou'wester off and we got a good look at him. He didn't look the sort who'd go to prep school. He was very pale, with marks under his eyes. He looked more the type that gets taken into Care.

'He said, "We get a train back to London for holidays. Mummy met me at Charing Cross. She said I mustn't be upset but Daddy had cleared the trees out of the hollow ready for planting the alpine garden. And I said he shouldn't have done that. I told him not to do it at Christmas but he said there were plenty of other places to play in the country, but there aren't. It's all sugar beet. I liked it when we lived in Cambridge; there were parks. I told Daddy not to cut down the oak tree because it was sacred."

'I thought, 'ere 'ere, pagan rites, but Sebastian says, "I thought he might leave it alone if I said it was sacred, but he said it was rotten. He said we'd plant a Japanese maple there if I minded so much, but the oak must go. So I had to tell the bees."

' "Are these imaginary bees, son?" Dave says, and

Sebastian says, "No. They were wild bees and they lived in a hole in the oak tree. I told them what Daddy was going to do."

' "Ho, yes," says Dave, the way you do when little kids talk about fairies at the bottom of the dustbin.

' "Don't you know about bees?" says Sebastian. "If you keep bees, you have to tell them things." '

'Bedtime stories?' Nina said.

'No,' Nazzer said. 'Our neighbours when we lived at Hoveton had a couple of hives. If anything important happened Mrs Hooper used to trot down the garden to tell the bees. We'd see her sometimes yakking away nineteen to the dozen, first thing in the morning, before the bees got up. She said they'd sulk otherwise. It wasn't election results, or international crises, just things like auntie popping off or the time they won on the Premium Bonds.'

'Oh, folk lore,' Nina said.

'Maybe, but he was a systems analyst and she wrote physics text books. You couldn't call them superstitious,' Nazzer said, 'but they had a lot of time for those bees.'

Maurice said, 'That's what Sebastian thought. He said he always told the bees if anything was going on and when he found that his dad was going to cut down their tree he went out and warned them. "They weren't hibernating," he said, "they were too savage for that, they were just asleep. It was a bit after Christmas and icy cold, but I went and woke them up. If you looked down the hole into the rotten bit you could see the old brown wax combs poking out. I broke a bit off as a signal and then I could hear them *growling*, right down inside the tree. But as soon as I spoke they knew it was me so they didn't come out." They were very fierce, he said, but they never stung *him*. Apparently they used to hang around the tree in summer and zap anyone who came near, just for kicks, not self defence, but never Sebastian. He said he told them they were in danger. He hoped they'd take the hint and fly away but of course, it was the wrong time of year for them to swarm, so they were still there when Daddy came along with his saw.

'His mum broke it to him while they were driving back from London. As soon as Daddy began sawing the bees woke up and started making threatening noises, what Sebastian called growling, so he went back to the house and got some kind of poison and poured it into the hollow. I don't know what it was but it finished off the bees. Next day he went out again, cut down the tree and burned the trunk.

' "Is that them there ashes?" Dave says. Sebastian says yes, and started crying again. We didn't know what to do, really. He wasn't the sort of little lad you could pat on the head and say there there to.

' "He burned the nest?" says Dave.

' "He burned the *bees*," says Sebastian. "They were in the tree and he burned them. Last year he poured boiling water on the *ants*. He poisoned the *moles*." I can tell you,' Maurice said, 'I was getting very glad this guy had swelled up. I said to Sebastian, "Look, if he put poison in the hole, the bees would have been dead before he burned them. They wouldn't have known about it."

' "They knew who did it though," Sebastian said. "I warned them. That's why they stung him."

' "When did they sting him?"

' "Yesterday," he says, "while Mummy was fetching me from London. He came out here with your friend Joe and they were waiting for him. I'm sorry they got Joe, but they never did like strangers." He climbed over my knees and got out of the Land Rover. It had stopped raining and he stood there in a puddle, looking in. "And they'll get you," he says. "You'd better keep away." And he ran off up the bank towards the bungalow. Dave looks at me and screws a finger into his forehead.

' "D'you reckon St Radigund's is a special school?" he says. I sort of shrugged. I mean,' Maurice said, 'I didn't think Sebastian was a nutter, but he gave me the creeps. "Oh well," says Dave, "let's get out and have a recce while the rain holds off," so we climbed out again and sloshed over to the oak stump. Sebastian had disappeared, it was all quiet except for water dripping off the shed. It was a little black tarred shack with a thatched roof.

' "We'll dig in underneath and loosen it a bit," Dave says. "Better take an axe to those roots." He stood back, the way you do before going into action, right into the middle of the pile of ash, and that was when we heard it.'

'Heard what?'

'Just like Sebastian said, a sort of growling, only it wasn't really growling but it was threatening, all right. And you couldn't tell where it was coming from, but it was close. Dave says, "What in heck is that?" and then he yelled and slapped the back of his neck and started flapping his arms. I knew what it was on account of Sebastian, but you could see how they'd taken Joe and old man Phillips by surprise. Then they started on me; I could feel them up my sleeves and down my neck; *crawling*. We both turned round and belted back to the Land Rover and the buzzing came with us. Dave got it worse than me because he'd been standing right in the middle of the ashes. What you might call the heart of the problem,' Maurice said. 'Live bees can only sting once, but after they're dead I suppose they can go on as long as they like. We sat in that Land Rover yelling and slapping like a pair of loonies and then Dave started it up and began to back out towards the road. You could hear the buzzing above the engine. It wasn't a sort of drowsy summer-day buzzing, either,' Maurice said. 'It was like Stukas. I looked out of the side window and there was Sebastian, back again, standing on the oak roots. Nothing was stinging *him*.

' "I'll tell old Phillips where he can put his tree stumps," says Dave, and the Land Rover's churning up mud behind like a muck spreader, and then just as we got clear, the shed collapsed. I thought for a moment we'd done it, I mean, that was impossible, but that's what it looked like. It came down slowly; first the thatch slid off all in a lump, and then the walls fell outwards, like someone had given the thing a shove from underneath. Of course, I guessed by then it was nothing to do with us at all, and I thought the rain must have washed away the foundations,' Maurice said, 'but once the walls were down you could see this mound in the middle where the floor should have been. It could have been a pile of compost, I suppose, but it looked more to me like a socking great mole hill.

'Dave saw it too. He revvs up and yells, "Let's get out of here before he calls in the ants!" I don't reckon Sebastian was telling the truth when he said that all his mates were at St Radigund's,' Maurice said. 'Not *all* of them.'

'It depends what you mean by mates,' Nazzer said.

The End of Silence

JOAN AIKEN

It was after Ma died that our father acquired the owl, and we started to hate him.

She was killed by a bomb. It happened at Frankfurt airport, when she was on her way back from a visit to Aunt Ginnie. 'Goodbye, see you next Saturday, I've left enough cooked food in the freezer for a week, and I'll try to bring back some German rock records,' she had said, when she left, six days earlier, and that was the last time we saw her. Death is extremely shattering when it comes baldly and unexpectedly like that; if somebody is ill, or in hospital, you have a little time to adjust, a little time for your mind to prepare. But in such a situation as ours, no way. I know this sounds obvious, but when you yourself are the victim, the truth of it really hits you.

We were all knocked out in different ways. My sister Helen went silent. I began addictively eating tortilla chips and reading murder mysteries. Bag after bag of chips, book after book, two or three a day. I got them from the local library or bought secondhand paperbacks from the Old Bus Station Wholesale Goods Mart. 'You'll get horribly fat if you don't stop,' Helen broke her silence to say. But I couldn't stop. Reading was a drug that numbed the pain.

Father came out worst. He went silent too, and lost a couple of stone in weight. Then he suddenly announced that he was sending us to boarding school.

His explanation *sounded* reasonable.

'I'm a writer, damn it! I've got to support us all and keep up the mortgage payments. My inventive faculty has to keep functioning, which is hard enough in present circumstances, lord knows. How do you think I'd manage if I had to keep remembering about things like fetching you from school and stew for dinner?'

Ma would have managed somehow, if she'd been the one who was left, I thought but didn't say. Helen pressed her lips together and stared at her feet and then turned and walked away.

Apart from the shock of losing all our friends and familiar surroundings at one sweep, the boarding school wasn't too bad. People knew what had happened to us and were kind without making a fuss. Our connection with Father was a help, I suppose. He is fairly well known because, besides being a poet and an expert on Anglo-Saxon, he wrote that book about Alfred and the Danes, *The King's Jewel*, which they did on television and it was very successful.

Which was one reason why we took his excuses for packing us off to boarding school with more than a pinch of salt.

'He just wants to get rid of us,' I said, 'because we remind him of Ma.'

'Well—he does have to look ahead,' Helen argued. 'One TV success won't last for ever. And it's four years since he wrote the *Jewel*. I'm sure he isn't doing any work. He just goes into the study and sits. I've seen him, through the window.'

'That's why he doesn't want us at home. He's afraid we'll ask what he's working on.'

When we went home for Christmas, there was the owl.

Aunt Joe had given it to Father. She's a vet, and someone had brought it into her surgery with a hurt wing, probably done by a car. 'Your father needs something to look after,' she told us. We would rather it had been us.

Walt Whitman was the name Aunt Joe had given the owl. It was a big bird, a pale barn owl, about a foot high, large as a cat, with a fawn-coloured back and skull feathers ending in a sort of Venus peak over its eyes. The rest of its feathers, front, face, and under-wings, were snowy white. The eyes were huge, black, and staring. I suppose it was a handsome beast, really, but we hated it. We felt it had supplanted us. There was something spooky and startling about its habits—you never knew where you would come across it suddenly, in the airing cupboard, or staring at you from the top of a bookshelf, or the handlebars of Helen's bike, or the kitchen dresser, or the oven. The oven and the medicine cupboard were two of its favourite spots.

'It's not hygienic!' Helen stormed at Father, but he said, 'Rubbish. Owls are very clean creatures. And Whitman has completely cleared this house of mice. There isn't one in the place nowadays.'

That was true. Mice had been a problem before. You do get them in old houses.

Whitman spent a lot of time in Father's study, perched on top of a bust of the poet Edgar Allan Poe. And because of this, Father insisted that we always knocked before going into the study—'So as not to startle Whitman.'

'Really I bet it's to give Father time to look as if he's been working,' Helen muttered.

But Father insisted that the owl *helped* him to work; its soundless presence in the room was an aid to concentration, he explained. I remembered that he used to say the same thing of Ma. 'The only person in the world whose being in the room didn't prevent me from thinking,' he had said about her, and sometimes he called her 'My gracious Silence'.

The owl affected our life in a good many ways. The landing window had to stay wide open at all times, rain or fine, hot or cold (and at Christmas it was *very* cold) for Whitman's comings and goings. The TV had to be turned off at ten sharp because, Father said, Whitman didn't care for the noise and vibration. Our friends with dogs were severely discouraged from coming to the house; in fact our friends were discouraged altogether; Whitman, said Father, didn't care for a lot of laughter and voices, or thumps and pop music, or smells of sausages and chips cooking. Whitman didn't like Helen practising the cello, according to Father, and he simply hated the sound of my trumpet.

'That bloody owl's just an excuse not to have us in the house at all!' Helen burst out one evening, close to furious tears because Father wouldn't let us give a party.

'Helen! I will not be spoken to like that! In any case I don't know how you can have the heart even to think of giving a party so soon after Marian—' His voice dried up and he sat staring at Helen with what seemed like hate.

'Don't you see, you silly man, it's because we want to take our minds *off*? How can we do that, when we have to tiptoe about all the time as if the place was an—an Intensive Care Unit?' And then Helen rushed out of the kitchen and up to her room, slamming doors all the way.

And Whitman, disturbed, left his perch on the plate rack and ghosted about the house on great pale wings, as if blown by an invisible gale.

Father simply stared at the calendar, obviously willing the last week of the holidays to go by at double-quick speed.

When we came home at Easter it was the same, only worse. Whitman was plainly fixed with us for life. Father had formed the habit of buying him little delicacies at a pet shop: foreign mice and lizards, things like that. The owl was more relaxed in our house; he made more noise than he had at Christmas, suddenly let out a weird shriek every now and then, which could startle you almost out of your wits. Or he would do a kind of loud snore, also very disconcerting, or suddenly snap his beak together with a loud click. He was not a restful house-mate. Despite this increase in vocal activity Father had, to our discomfort, begun to address the owl as Silence. Whitman, he said, was a silly name, not suitable, not dignified. Besides, Whitman was a silly poet. Silence was much more suitable.

All the old rules and regulations were in force, and some new ones too. Transistors were totally banned, so was playing table tennis. Father was afraid that Silence might get over-excited and swallow one of the balls, which could kill him.

'I wish it would,' said Helen furiously. 'If Father were to *marry* again, I suppose I'd hate it, but at least it would be possible to understand, and sympathize, because he's lonely and—and unfulfilled; at least that would be *natural*. But to be tyrannized over by a beastly *owl* —that's just absolutely *un*natural and spooky—it's like something out of those Poe tales that Father used to read us.'

In the old days, when Ma was alive, we all used to read aloud to each other quite a lot; now we never did any more. I daresay, if pressed, Father would have been able to come up with some reason why Whitman —Silence—wouldn't like it.

'Do you think we could kidnap Whitman?' I suggested. 'Pick a time when Father's out of the house, put the beast in a basket, and take him off on our bikes to some distant spot, and leave him there?'

'We could try,' said Helen.

So we tried. We rode twenty miles—to Cranfield Forest—and left Whitman on an oak stump.

He was home before we were. So that was no good.

'Owls are very place-oriented,' Helen said. She had been reading about them in the bird book. 'They use the same nest year after year. Obviously Whitman looks on this house as his nest now . . .'

'Well then I think we have to murder him.'

'*Murder* him!' Helen looked aghast; but then she looked thoughtful.

For days we went around without speaking; we were all of us obsessed by the owl, one way or another. The awful thing was that he did, in some way, remind me of Ma; there was something about his pale face and widow's-peak brown cap and great dark eyes that somehow called up her face, but in a teasing, horrible, unreal way. I suppose that may have been at the bottom of his fascination for Father.

I spent hours racking my brain to think of some foolproof way to get rid of the owl. It would have to be done without the least chance of arousing Father's suspicion, or the results would be dreadful: he'd probably kick us back to school and forbid our coming home at all, send us to labour camps in the holidays and never speak to us again. But really, for his welfare as much as ours, I thought the deed must be done, only how? Poison, for instance, was out of the question; anything of that kind would point to us.

One night, after thrashing about wide awake for hours, I got up long before dawn. I sat hunched on my wide windowsill, gazing out. Our house lay on the edge of the town and beyond our garden hedge was a big hundred-acre field of young winter wheat, beginning to grow thick and green; beyond that lay a little wood. The sun, on the right, came up into a dim red cloudy sky like a thin melon-slice of blazing gold; into this theatrical light came a buoyant flitting shape which I soon recognized as Whitman, methodically quartering the wheat-field for breakfast. He flew quite silently, coasting with very little effort; then, every so often, suddenly dropped with a wild flapping of wings. I've read that a barn owl can bring back a mouse to the nest every fifteen minutes. I don't think Whitman caught as many as that; but then he had no chicks to feed. The situation was unnatural for him too. Seen flying, his body looked wedge-shaped, and the wide pale wings looked almost translucent with the marmalade-coloured sunlight coming through them. And then, Mother's face looking out between them, when he turned his big black eyes in my direction . . . He has *got* to go, I thought, though at that moment I felt quite sad about it; he was so handsome, coasting to and fro in the early light that, just then, I felt a kind of sympathy with Father. All the same, he has to go, or we shall end up stark crazy.

It was at that moment I had the idea how to do it.

Father was due to go up to Edinburgh that day, to receive an honorary degree from the university. No cash in it, just bags of honour, he said rather drily. Still, it would be beneficial for him to get away, the first time he had done so since Ma's death, and he would stay a night in Edinburgh and return the following day.

He gave us endless instructions.

'Don't forget to lock up, last thing. And make sure all the lights are out. And mind you leave the landing window open, so that Silence can fly in and out.'

At least we didn't have to worry about feeding Silence; he was a pet who provided his own diet, to do him justice. Though I didn't doubt Father would bring him back some fancy tit bit from Scotland, Celtic mice or Caledonian lizards. Whitman's presents at Christmas had far outnumbered ours, which consisted of an obviously last-minute chemistry set and paintbox.

Father left only just in time because road-works were in progress along our stretch of lane: a new water main was being laid, there were men with drills and a great excavator and a stretch of muddy trench on one side of the road, and a long lumpy ridge where the completed ditch had been filled in. The sound of the digger and the pneumatic drills had been steadily coming closer for the past three days; Whitman hated it, and so did Father; he was really delighted to get away to Edinburgh, and particularly today, when the work would be right out-side our house. In fact if he had delayed his departure by another ten minutes the men would have dug their trench right across our garage entrance and he would have had to make his journey by bus and train.

We never kissed each other for greetings or farewells any more. 'Behave yourselves,' Father called, flapping his hand out of the car window, and then he drove away quickly, under the snout of the digger, which was just getting itself into position.

'Where's Whitman?' I said to Helen, as we put away the breakfast dishes.

'In the pantry. Why?'

'I've had the perfect idea. Come on: we'll do it now, and then we'll go out for the day. Take a picnic to Bardley Down. The house is going to be unbearable all day, anyway, with that row outside.'

We found Whitman dozing on the pantry top shelf. He did that most of the day, sometimes snoring, as I have said.

By now he was quite used to us, and only snarled and grunted a bit as I picked him up and sat him in the gas oven, on the lowest rack, having taken out the others. Then I shut the door and turned on the gas.

After that, feeling like murderers—as we were—we grabbed some cheese and apples, locked front and back doors, and fled from the place.

'There won't be any sign of how he died,' I said. 'Father can't possibly guess. He'll probably think Whitman died of old age. After all, we have no idea how old he is.'

'Father will be horribly upset,' Helen said wretchedly.

'Maybe that will be good for him.'

'Just so long as he doesn't go and get another owl . . .'

We had a ghastly day. It was cold and cloudy, not quite raining, but raw; we had brought along books in our packs, but it was too cold to stop and read them, so we walked and walked, in a huge circle, and ate our lunch standing, in a big yew forest where the trees gave us a bit of shelter, leaning against one of the big reddish trunks. At one point we heard the unmistakable screech of an owl—'Yik, yik!' in the gloom.

'Whitman would have liked it here,' Helen said sadly.

'It's no use, Nell. You know he'd only have come boomeranging back. We did try . . .'

At last, more dead than alive, we limped home ourselves, just as dusk was beginning to fall.

We had planned what to do: open doors and windows to let the gas escape, then retreat to the greenhouse for twenty minutes. The greenhouse was kept at an even temperature by an oil heater; it was the first time we had been warm all day.

'The gas ought to have dispersed by now,' I said finally.

So we went cautiously indoors and flung open lots more windows. I turned off the gas and opened the oven door just a crack. I didn't look inside the oven. Hadn't the heart. Thought I'd wait till morning.

'I'm going up to bed,' I said. 'Don't feel like supper.'

'Me too. Is it safe to go to sleep, though?'

'Open your bedroom window wide. And don't go striking any matches.'

We crept to bed. I had expected to lie awake, racked by guilt and horror at the deed we had done. But I didn't; I slept as if I had been karate-chopped.

It was Helen who lay awake. When she came down in the morning I was alarmed: she was whiter than Whitman's shirt-front.

'Ned! *Whitman has been haunting me all night*!' she croaked. 'He's been perched on my bed-rail!'

'Oh, come on!' I said. But I was pretty scared myself—not of ghosts; I thought Helen was having some kind of breakdown. She looked so white and wild and trembling that I wondered if I ought to call the doctor.

'He made me think of Mother!' Helen wept. 'Oh, Ned—why in the world did we do it?'

Just then Whitman—or his ghost—came coasting into the room on silent wings.

'Keep him away—keep him off me!' Helen shrieked.

Whitman made for the oven—the door of which stood open. And that made me realize for the first time that there was *no corpse inside*.

'It's all right, you dope—he's *not dead*.'

At that moment there came a peal at the front door.

'Gas inspector,' said the man who stood there. 'I've come to reconnect you and check.'

'Reconnect—?'

'Didn't you know? The excavator cut the gas main yesterday. All this row of houses were cut off. Hey, what the blooming—?'

He had suddenly come face to face with Whitman, sitting in the oven.

'Oh, that's our owl,' I said, weak and idiotic with relief. 'He, he likes sitting there.'

'Pretty stupid, dangerous place to let him sit,' said the gas man. 'Unless you fancy roast owl.'

And he went about his business of reconnecting and testing.

That day we stayed at home. Our spirit was broken. We endured the hideous row made by the excavator and the drills—a few yards farther along, now; we did our school holiday work and washed some clothes; I mowed the lawn, Helen made a shepherd's pie against Father's return. That meant turning Whitman out of the oven. Restless and displeased, he found himself a new perch on the front hall coat-rack. I suppose being shut inside the oven had insulated him nicely, the day before, from the noise of the drills and the thuds of the digger.

'I hope they don't cut the gas main again,' said Helen. 'I'm dying for a bath.'

At tea time, Father came home. Cross and tired, he flung open the front door—and Whitman flew out, straight into the jaws of the excavator. One crunch, and he was done for . . .

Father and Helen wept in one another's arms.

'He was so like Mother,' she sobbed. 'He had just her way of looking at you and not saying anything—'

'Yes, yes, I know, I know—'

Father didn't blame us. How could he? The death of Silence was nobody's fault.

But of course we feel just as guilty as if we had really murdered him. After all, we meant to; it was pure chance that our intentions came to nothing. We really are murderers.

Helen seems to have washed away her guilt in tears, and in looking after Father. But I haven't: I suppose because the gas oven was my idea. And I suppose it is because of that guilt that Whitman haunts me and not Helen.

Night after night, there he is, perched on my bed-rail, silent, motionless, staring at me with Mother's eyes. Whether I'm at school or at home, it makes no difference. Nobody else sees him.

Strangely enough, I'm starting to grow rather fond of him.

Some Common Misunderstandings About Ghosts

RONALD FRAME

First things first. If you don't believe that ghosts exist, I'd skip this story and go on to the next one.

1 *That ghosts don't have a sense of humour. (Also, that ghosts are seen but not heard.)*

You know the usual kind, mooning about with a fit of the miseries, and the only fun they can manage comes from shaking their arms and frightening people who're doing *them* no harm, just trying to get a decent night's sleep in what they thought was a common-or-garden four-poster bed.

I heard of a family who moved into an old house. There were wooden beams, leaded casement windows, a beard of red Virginia creeper covering the front. Inside the house at night the joists and floorboards twitched and creaked; the grandfather clock on the staircase landing ticked with particular, s-l-o-w seriousness; birds—or mice—made scuttling sounds up in the roof.

Of course, a legend went with the house, that there was a ghost: and certainly the house seemed to be *made* for one. The mother and father and their three children lay awake for the first few nights: they'd once lived in an old Cornish rectory, and on squally nights when rain was thrown at the windows and the gutters and rainpipes rattled, a moaning would fill the rooms of the house, doors would open and close—not loudly, with banging, but very softly, the latches lifting lightly and then clicking shut. The next morning certain objects would be found to be in not *quite* the same position they had been in the night before when the lights were switched off. So the family knew what to expect in their new home, and—almost as a courtesy—they pinched themselves awake for the first four or five nights awaiting a visitation from the spirit: surely the ghost was interested in seeing what the house's latest occupants were like?

It didn't appear, however. They guessed it must have a surprise up its sleeve, to keep them—as it were—on their toes.

But it *still* didn't make an appearance. The family weren't aware of it until the first of the year's good weather came, when they were all outside playing croquet—or attempting to play croquet, not by any proper rules—on the front lawn. Everyone was laughing, the parents were leaning on their mallets helpless with mirth at the spectacle—when it suddenly struck each of the five of them at exactly the same moment, there was a sixth source of laughter!

A child's laughter.

Their own laughs trailed away, the parents' then the children's, then—last of all—the intruder's.

It was perplexing. Everyone looked at one another. There was a choked giggle from behind them, followed by silence.

Another day, a couple of weeks later, the children heard the laughter again. They were playing on the staircase with a trio of friends who'd come visiting with their parents. The game was for two of them at a time to race each other to the bottom, one running and jumping downstairs and the other sliding down the banister. The hall echoed with their laughter. The two sets of parents were outside in the garden, so there were no limits to the amount of noise they could make. Perhaps it was odd then that over the laughs and shouts of their own six voices they could hear a seventh. But somehow they did, and—again—they listened to their voices trailing away, till only the invisible stranger's was left.

Then silence.

In the seconds and minutes afterwards no one was particularly frightened by what had happened, except perhaps the two youngest. The stranger had sounded cheerful, relaxed, as if she (it was a girl, they all agreed) was only wanting to share in their high jinks. The visitors, speaking low and furtively, asked where the laughter had come from: the children who lived in the house shrugged their shoulders, and looked—the visitors decided later—less concerned than they might be. Was it a trick?

No, it wasn't a trick. It happened again, a number of times that summer, always when the family were least expecting that it would, when they were at their most carefree, thinking of nothing else than their own amusement: playing croquet, shaking apples from the trees, planning model-train lay-outs round the furniture in one of the bedrooms, trying on some flappers' party clothes from the 1920s which they found in a dusty trunk in the attic. It was as the children were dressing up that the mysterious laughter became loudest, happiest. When *their* laughter stopped, the stranger's continued for several seconds later.

The family never *saw* the child who laughed. When they enquired about the legend of a ghost, they discovered that a girl had lived in the house long before, in the first years of the new century. A sad thing happened —they usually do in ghost stories—when she was eight years old the child fell ill, and at the end of a long summer she died.

The ghost, the family realized, wished them no harm, no frights. She was merely looking to find her own lost childhood, and to take part in the pleasure of the three childhoods being lived in the house *now*. The house held no mischief for the family. In time they came to anticipate the ghost-child's presence, on hot cloudless summer days in the holidays when there was no school. She stood watching over their shoulders, and saw the fun *she*'d never had. In a way she was living *through* them. It was always when their enjoyment was heartiest that she appeared, their summer ghost, when they were all in an easy frame of mind.

Sometimes, running out into the garden, the children would remember, and turn and look backwards, as if waiting. They never *saw* anything. The child laughed at the magic tricks Matthew had picked up from a book, but they thought *her* magic was in a different class altogether, how she could travel across the garden after them and make no sound or run behind them at 'tag' and never be foot-faulted or brushed against.

2 *That ghosts only haunt old buildings.* (*Also, that they don't like pop music.*)

The Black Tulip discothèque was sited in the basement of a smart hi-tech block in the centre of the city. You entered through automatic smoked-glass doors from the street, passed a hat-check counter, then were conducted downstairs in a gleaming stainless-steel lift.

When the lift doors opened again, the sight of the night-club took most people's breath away. Neon lights flashed and rippled; a waterfall dropping through the roof changed colour every few seconds; in another rainbow-coloured tank a girl dressed as a mermaid splashed about; several video screens high on the walls showed films as well as shots of the clientele as they emerged from the lift; the disc jockey and video jockey operated the electronic equipment from two cages, which were suspended fifteen or twenty feet above the dance floor and moved across the ceiling on a system of rails.

The people who came went to great lengths dressing for an evening in the most way-out discothèque in the city. They wore the most outlandish clothes they could find or devise for themselves. Some had a space theme—silver robot-suits, forty-first-century plastic astronaut outfits—and others were exotic in different ways: someone always wore an unwieldy bear-skin with the head attached (he resembled, of all things, a Roman centurion), a woman was allowed to enter (only after a vet's certificate of approval was shown) with a snake wound round her waist, while another woman would come covered in feathers; others wore ripped and shredded clothes in carefully toning colours, and resembled nothing so much as particularly elegant scarecrows; one woman liked to dress in a cat's costume, with holes in the mask for her mouth and nose and eyes. Hair came in all shades, silver, scarlet, lemon; faces varied from the palest of pale to others bedecked in make-up and as colourful as an artist's palette. The motto of the Black Tulip discothèque, which it used on its publicity, was 'Anything goes—and everyone who is *any*one comes!' In the city it was *the* place for the young and fashionable to be seen: that is, if they could afford to come—and those who couldn't really afford it would forget about eating for a couple of days if they could save the money that way.

Well, what does all this have to do with ghosts, you might ask? I'm coming to that. I have to establish the background first, which might be the last place you would expect to find . . .

But—permit me—a little history by way of preparation, unappreciated by most of the clientele of the Black Tulip discothèque, who gyrated to the jungle beat in blissful, happy-headed ignorance of the fact that they were amusing themselves on the spot where others, generations before, had similarly enjoyed a dance of an evening: Victorians in a pompous town hall, Georgians in an airy blue-and-white assembly room, Elizabethans in the commodious town-house of a noble baron of the realm.

It was into the Black Tulip discothèque, not long after it opened in the basement of the impressive smoked-glass and terrazzo edifice rising ten floors above, that there walked the Lady Matilda Sizewaggon. It was an unfortunate surname to possess, even in the second half of the sixteenth century: Lady Matilda was in fact lean, petite, lithe. She had always kept herself in good shape, riding in the country where she lived, eating sensibly, and—her favourite occupation when she was in town, staying at her brother-in-law's fine house—dancing to viols and lutes. She enjoyed all dances—pavans, galliards, almains (when everybody leapt up in the air)— and she couldn't resist the lure of music.

It was the music for the dance that had brought her back, time and time again: the Georgians' cotillions and quadrilles, the Victorians' Viennese polkas and waltzes, the twenties' tangos and foxtrots. Now, in the newest days of the Black Tulip, she wasn't so sure about things. *But*, she did know very well, fashions change and it was up to her to adjust.

What she enjoyed best about the Black Tulip was being unknown there and being able to blend in with the crowd. Never seeing the light of day, she felt herself dreadfully pallid and ashen after four hundred years, but she realized she didn't have to worry: among certain patrons of the place, it seemed to be the required 'look'. She wore her wide silk gown and pleated ruff collar, since they were all she had to stand up in, but usually no one gave them a second glance: except those women who appeared to envy her her 'dress sense'. A couple of times people had tried to start conversations with her— 'what lovely material!', 'is that a *real* ruff round your neck?'—but she'd managed to smile and pass on without having to speak, in her own language that would have sounded so strange to them.

But could any strangeness *she* was capable of outdo the Black Tulip? She doubted it. The lights and activity amused her, they kept her entertained when she couldn't sleep. 'Arise and join them' was *her* motto, whatever the Black Tulip's happened to be. So thither she would wend her way, and hover on the fringes of the gathering, a little afraid to dance—although occasionally the music *could* persuade her, and she swayed in time, just a little, gently. The dance beats were rather different from those of her own time, but in that far-off age the continent of Africa had only been a dark wonder to them. She would ponder, how many old-fashioned tabors might it have taken to produce that same drum effect?

At the Black Tulip she was in fact more at her ease—whatever minor reservations she might have had —than she had been for the past four centuries. The clientele continued to fascinate her, with their fancy dress. Sometimes she'd have a silly notion that she should talk to some of them: *she* could certainly tell them a thing or two! But ghosts, have you noticed, often prefer to keep their silence, just to watch and say nothing. Why, I wonder? If they were to speak too much (which is the temptation, or the risk, after being silent for so long) maybe the words would turn into weights, chains, like an anchor—the worst could happen, they might start to make friends with you!—and how then could they just get up and go, as ghosts always do, leave with a smile, float free, pass through the nearest available wall back into their mystery?

3 *That your great-aunt can't be a ghost.*

Oh yes, she can. Like the Great-Aunt Sedilia of someone I heard about.

(*Also, are you really one person, or half a person, or two people?*)

I don't think she was crazy. She was quite grand, and believed people should behave properly. She never allowed her spine to touch the back of the chair when she was sitting at the table eating; she distrusted a man if he rolled his shirt sleeves past the elbow (that meant he wasn't a gentleman); she thought certain women of her generation (the early Suffragettes) were much too pushy and noisy.

But there was another Great-Aunt Sedilia. Or, rather, she imagined there was another version of herself. She had the notion that everyone is born into this world half-complete, that there is another half you have to quest for and find in order to become a whole and finished person. She was a woman without envy, except where twins were concerned. Twins were the two halves of a whole: they were complete in themselves. When a woman married a man, then each had a chance of becoming complete (if they were well matched, of course): two halves will make up the whole, although sometimes they were unequal portions, because she knew some very weak-willed wives and some very wishy-washy husbands.

She herself hadn't married. She didn't think a man *could* be her other half: she had gone to a girls' school, she had been brought up by her mother and grandmother and had lived among aunts and great-aunts, so how could she hope to understand how a man's mind operated? It was impossible.

Nonetheless, she didn't let that stop her searching. She didn't think she could marry, and she knew she didn't have a twin sister or brother; none of her friends seemed to have quite the qualities she was looking for.

'All my life,' she announced one day to the family of her niece and her husband (she owned the house, but they shared it with her), 'I've been imagining who my other half might be.' For years, she told them, she had tried imagining just where in the world her other half was to be found, in which country and continent. 'Now I think it's time for me to find out.'

And with that she gave notice of her impending departure, duly made her preparations, and left the town and England.

She searched in many countries. She wrote saying she thought she had found her other half, not so far away in fact, in a little town in Holland: a lock-keeper's wife who bore a definite resemblance to herself, and who spoke to her as if—how odd it was!—as if they'd been friends all their lives. But something must have disappointed Great-Aunt Sedilia finally because the next communication they had from her came from Turkey, from Istanbul: she'd met someone, a man this time, who looked a little like her father and who did everything she might have done if she'd been born a boy—he worked in some sort of business her own father had made his living at, he wore the clothes she liked best to see men in, he enjoyed activities she had some respect for, such as taking photographs, swimming backwards, being able to cultivate orchids in a greenhouse. But that too in the end seemed *not* to be the answer she was looking for.

At long last however she *did* have her wish fulfilled, and she found the person she believed was her other half. The woman lived in, of all places, an Indian village in the dusty back of beyond. Apparently she was very poor, but she showed a serene and placid attitude to everything: she had great dignity, she walked like a princess, was generous in giving things and in her opinions about other people as only—so Great-Aunt Sedilia wrote—'as only a poor person can be'.

The family at home realized something must be badly wrong with their relative. At the age of fifty she should have known better, but apparently she didn't. She wrote from India to say she was going to stay in that country, in the village, in the wilds, for a while longer.

At home everyone was stunned by the news. They hardly liked to speak about her and what she'd done. Another letter was received, saying she had now adjusted better to the heat, she was very happy living in this way, she thought she would stay on longer. In yet another letter that 'longer' became 'indefinitely'.

Ghosts come in different kinds. They don't all fly down corridors, or play childish pranks, throwing things round the room. Ghosts can be imagined out of *someone not being there*, where you think they should be.

Great-Aunt Sedilia's family all considered themselves level-headed. But each of them started to *see* the lady, when they knew—in their brains—that she couldn't be there. No one saw her in the same place. Her niece occasionally caught sight of her in Harrods, in haberdashery or the food halls; her niece's husband glimpsed her walking in the garden as she used to do, examining the roses; her niece's children thought they heard her moving about the rooms of her old home—now *their* home—in the middle of the night.

It was as if, they all separately told themselves, she was trying to tell them something: that the stiff, straight-backed Sedilia Brooke who'd given them the 'rules' of their lives hadn't known everything, that maybe it wasn't the most important thing in the world that you should keep up 'appearances', that you should be seen to be this or that, always correctly turned out: would it have mattered if she'd let her spine touch the back of the dining-chair now and then?

Great-Aunt Sedilia's ghost seemed to be saying: 'See the world, see how other people live their lives'. Instead, though, her family became embarrassed about her. Her niece and her husband went to great lengths making up excuses to 'explain' her behaviour. Her great-nephews and -nieces found it easier to make jokes about her, and to tell them to their friends. Later on, however, a silence on the subject was observed in the house—it was considered a simpler solution to the problem—and so the red faces and harsh giggles became unnecessary.

Great-Aunt Sedilia's brass name-plate was taken off the great front door. The telephone was re-registered in her niece's husband's name. It seemed the best policy, just to forget about her. But the family's guilt at their own behaviour didn't let them forget everything and the lady's ghost with the ramrod back was a constant reminder, that they shouldn't think the job of being themselves and knowing who they were was over and finished: *that* job is never done, the search to know everything about yourself lasts all your life, and sometimes longer. But this is getting complicated.

4 *That ghosts always belong to the past.* (*Also, that a ghost is always someone else, not yourself.*)

Let's call her Sarah. Imagine an old house in a high-walled summer garden: there's plenty of space to lose yourself in, outside and indoors.

This is the Edwardian age (a very ghostly period, incidentally—remember the laughing child who died). For people of Sarah's and her mother's station in life, demure manners are an obligation, and the proper clothes or 'attire', and discreet customs like calling-cards when visits are made and dance-cards at balls, to be filled in next to the dance in question with the name of whichever young man has had the courage to ask for the pleasure of your company.

Sarah thinks it all pretty much rot, if the truth be told, (which of course, according to her mother, always *should* be told.) This particular day she's in one of her rebellious moods, which her widowed mother finds so difficult to cope with. They have come to call on the Frobishers, whose fine house sits in this blooming garden. They have come, Sarah is fully aware, with a purpose. At sixteen years old she understands that 'plans', although still somewhat vague, are being made for her future: with no father in the natural position of command, her mother has the task of attending to another ritual of the age, the search for a suitable beau for her daughter.

Sarah excuses herself from the group in the garden— her mother, Mr and Mrs Frobisher, and their son, whom she has scarcely as much as glanced at (he's pleasant-looking, and quiet, but she doesn't allow that to be either here or there)—and she goes indoors to the bathroom. To cool herself she dabs her face with luke-warm water she scents with lavender soap, and she peers long and hard at her reflection in the mirror set deep in the heavy, dark-stained mahogany panelling.

If I had the space to tell you the whole story—and if it wasn't just as important that I should tell you how Sarah felt afterwards—I should go through it stage by stage by stage: Sarah opening doors and looking into rooms, catching sight of the others outside through the windows and thinking it wrong that in 1908 young people shouldn't be permitted to make up their own minds about who their future husband or wife should be.

At some point she was drawn upstairs. Ahead of her she caught movements.

'Hello?' she said, thinking she was trespassing and was about to be discovered.

Something made her follow, however, even though she might be out of bounds. A woman was always walking just out of her range of vision, passing into different rooms and out again.

'Hello?' she repeated, but more timidly.

The woman was wearing a strange dress; its hem reached half way up her calf.

Sarah was puzzled. She continued to follow. Only once did she see the woman's face, fleetingly, as she turned off into the last room on the corridor: the features were curiously familiar to her, although she couldn't think whose they were, not at first.

Sarah tapped on the door jamb, and waited—a little breathlessly—for a reply.

She tapped again.

Nothing.

She looked inside. There was no one there inside the room. And no other door. Only a window, closed against the midsummer heat.

She wanted to smile with disbelief, but couldn't. She shook her head. Drops of perspiration were dribbling down her back, in the groove of her spine.

Then—as if willed into the room, not of her own choosing—she felt her legs carrying her (they *must* be my legs, she was thinking) towards a table-top.

Her eyes grew in her head and stared at what she saw.

Framed photographs.

Of a garden like the one outside. Of a girl like herself, standing with a woman like her mother. The Frobishers were in another photograph—father, mother, son. In a larger one the young woman and the young man stood outside a church, arm-in-arm, as wife and husband. The young man alone, seated, looked out of a silver frame, wearing military uniform.

Sarah shook her head, then suddenly stared behind her at the door: it was still open, she only had to walk through it to escape . . .

She turned round again. Her eyes lingered on the objects in the room and registered them to remember later: a wooden box with a round mesh grille in it—a bizarre apparatus filled with gauze and with a tap on its front, set into the fireplace—a table lamp with a fringed cloth shade and a long plaited tail trailing from it, leading to a point low on the wall, on the skirting board— another very queer instrument, a black stand on a table top, holding something like a scaled-down speaking tube.

Step by step, Sarah backed out of the room.

Where had the woman disappeared to? Who was she?—a mad inventor? What was the meaning of the photographs, laid out with such care, such pride?

The girl—now nearly a young woman—walked backwards into sunshine, which fell in a wide dusty shaft through the window at the end of the corridor: the sunshine of her summer's day, in this year of God's grace 1908.

I suppose I should say that Sarah was terribly upset and distressed by the experience but, if the truth be told (as her mother always insisted), she couldn't really believe it had happened.

Walking back downstairs, it seemed to her it might *not* have happened: or rather, it was as if she'd had a dream—she'd fallen asleep on top of a bed, and woken up. Or the heat and the giddiness inside her head and the white spots dancing in front of her eyes were to blame. She'd thought she'd seen someone *who might have been herself*, grown into an adult: in a year far beyond this one, living in a house she had the sole responsibility of running, on the other side of a great war.

She stood in the middle of the hall, unsteady on her feet. She felt the damp chill on her back under her clinging gingham. She concentrated all that she could, listening for sounds upstairs.

She could hear nothing.

But then she remembered, from every spooky story

88

she'd read, wasn't it the case that ghosts never as much as cause a floorboard to creak?

The question is, if you were able to see the future in front of you, could you do anything in the here and now to change it?

What can Sarah do when she returns to the garden, where her mother is being entertained to tea under a cedar tree by the Frobishers, where Edward Frobisher sits with his parents, looking thoroughly miserable?

It is no easier for *him*, she realizes with what story-tellers forever call 'a pang of the heart'.

Is it possible that he will die while he's still in his youth?—in a horrific war? As she walks towards the group, she keeps her eyes fixed on him.

Because she can imagine what will happen is no reason to let her present time be determined by it, she knows that. But she also knows that she has been too much blinded by her proud prejudices to be aware of anything other than *her* own pleasure.

Her mother has understood very well that she has seen through her plans. Maybe that is sufficient victory for Sarah, for the moment. The others meanwhile seem pleased by her return. She smiles in their direction, awkwardly.

'We were concerned for you, Sarah dear,' Mr Frobisher says as he rises to his feet.

'Have you had a little walk?' his wife enquires, very nicely. 'Did you go far?'

Into the future, Sarah answers to herself. Crazily. Was it possible?

Edward Frobisher has sensitive hands: she examines them while she pretends—rather woozily—to be adjusting the position of her chair. She falls on to the cushion, feeling almost faint; weakly she fans a fly from her face.

Suddenly, with no warning, she sees Edward

Frobisher's hands caked with trench mud, bloody and stiff with cold.

She pulls herself up in the chair. Her head hurts but it is beginning to clear.

Why, she asks herself indignantly as she looks at each of the group in turn, why can't people be allowed to get on with living their lives? Mother, me, Mr and Mrs Frobisher, their poor unsuspecting son? Why does history have to decide for us? Even the accident that killed Father had to do with history: if the train hadn't been so busy that day with sightseers going up to London to watch Queen Victoria's Jubilee procession, he might not have gone by road, and then the trap wouldn't have been hit by the runaway horse and Father sent tumbling on to the cobblestones.

She knows, dimly, that it's wrong to let sympathy decide for her the issue of who her future husband will be. She won't let it, she tells herself. Instead—she draws herself up straight in her chair, smiles at her mother who smiles back, clearly surprised by the gesture—instead she will be *fair* in her judgments. That is one thing she understands on this most unlikely afternoon, made for white rabbits and Cheshire cats.

'I will be fair,' she whispers to herself, under her breath, as she accepts a teacup and saucer from their hostess.

'Thank you,' she says in a voice that can just be heard and no more.

She still doesn't approve of 'arranged marriages' in this day and age, the ghostly high summer of 1908 they're living through, but as for Edward Frobisher—yes, she decides, yes, he *will* be given his chance.

Green Gravel

JILL PATON WALSH

'What about that?' the woman said, pointing at the card in the estate agent's window.

'You want to go back to school?' the man said, smiling.

'Nothing else here looks even possible,' she said. 'Do look, Mark.'

'Development opportunity,' he read. 'The Old School House, Ravensway, with planning permission for conversion to a four-bedroomed luxury detached home . . .'

'It's pretty,' she said. 'Nice new thatch. I like the belfry on the roof. It's got a little land; not too much. And I think I remember us driving through Ravensway last year, and liking the look of it.'

'Hmm,' he said. 'I suppose the Education Committee will have kept the basic fabric in good repair. Lots of room. Could be good. OK, let's go and look.'

'You go in and fix it while I hop across the road and buy us a picnic,' she said. 'We'll be starving otherwise.'

'I'm starving now,' he said.

Returning to the car with a bulging plastic bag she said, 'I got French bread, and paté, and tomatoes. Will that keep the wolves at bay?'

'Lovely. It's unoccupied. A Miss Flewin right next door has the keys. She's expecting us.'

'Off we go then.'

But they didn't go straight there. They drove round Ravensway, sussing it out, finding the village shop, the

Post Office, the little railway station. They ate their lunch on a sagging bench under a chestnut tree, on the village green, eyeing in the distance the School House under its cosy brown thatch, taking their time, getting the feel of the place. A deeply quiet feel. A good contrast with the frenetic life they led in town.

Mark spread out the plans the estate agent had given him. They frowned over them, trying to make sense of the faint blue lines.

'I don't think so,' he said. 'It would be nicer to leave the space open to the roof, don't you think? Come on, eat up. I'm getting interested in this.'

'First find Miss Flewin,' she said, standing up, brushing crumbs from her skirt.

Miss Flewin's house was easily found. The School House itself overlooked the green, standing well back, and a few yards further up the lane, a tiny gabled house in similar bricks, with similar distinctive pointed windows stood guard over the escapes from the erstwhile playground to a patch of enticing, promising woodland.

'Miss Flewin has what was once the schoolmistress's house,' said Mark, assessing it. They knocked on the sun-cracked, green-painted door.

Nobody came. They stood waiting, mildly disconcerted. A bird sang rapturously in the wood behind the gables. Mark tried again.

'Perhaps she was expecting us sooner. Perhaps we shouldn't have taken time for lunch. Really, we've been very leisurely about it.'

'Bother!' said Mark. 'I shall be very disappointed if . . .'

He banged the door again, and as he did so they could hear a faint sound within the house, a door opening, footfalls, someone coming after all.

You could see why she was slow the moment you caught sight of her. A very old, very frail lady, thin and tall in spite of her stoop, seeming to be made of bones and cardigan, with a lovely ancient tortoiseshell comb in her upswept white hair. A diaphanous halo of fine strands escaped the comb, and surrounded her deeply wrinkled face. A pair of disconcertingly sharp lilac-blue eyes stared at an uptilted angle—for really she was very stooped—at her visitors.

The woman felt at once ashamed, ashamed they had banged three times, vulgarly, bossily, in the presence of such self-possession.

'Mr Chittenden? You'll be Mr Chittenden,' said Miss Flewin, 'and Mrs Chittenden . . .'

'And thank God I am,' the woman thought, a sudden perception making her shudder at what she would have been, otherwise, in the cold lilac eyes of Miss Flewin.

'You have the keys of the Schoolhouse, I believe,' Mark was saying.

'I'll get them,' the old lady said, 'and I'll just get my shoes on.'

'Oh, but surely . . .' said Mark. But he was addressing the bent back of Miss Flewin as she shuffled slowly away down her hall, sliding her worn slippers on the lino.

He pulled a face at his wife. He was fidgeting, longing to get the keys in his hands and get into the school. He was quick at everything: quick moving, quick thinking, quick to act. It was agony for him to wait for people; long ago she had learnt to say, 'Go without me,' or, 'I'll catch up.'

And now they were caught, suspended. They could hardly walk into the open door of the house, and demand the keys. They could equally hardly abandon the quest and walk away . . . The bird sang frantically, as though busking a waiting crowd. 'It's a lovely situation,' she said in a while, filling time.

'Oh, I've got high hopes,' he said. 'If the inside is promising this could be it; don't you think so, Jean?'

'I saw it first,' she said, smugly. 'I liked it first.'

93

'This is maddening!' he cried, in a while longer. 'Wherever has that crazy old biddy got to?'

'Hush, hush, she might hear you! She's putting on her shoes.'

'But we don't want her trailing along . . .'

Mark was always constrained, formal, with strangers. Only alone with her had she ever seen him real. Of course he wanted to see over the building, discuss what to do with it, without the tedious Miss Flewin. Just the same she shushed him.

'Oh, she's bound to be deaf!' he said. But, Jean thought, just in case she's not . . . I'm a bit afraid of her.

'She has that in her face I would fain serve . . .' she murmured.

'What's that?' said Mark, treading on the spot, like one treading water.

'Authority . . .' she said. But it was no good playing quotations with Mark.

'Oh, do come on!' he said to the absent Miss Flewin.

And she still took so much longer that he couldn't bear it. 'I'll take a closer look at the outside, I think,' he said, and strode away, almost running down the lane, and disappearing towards the school gate.

Miss Flewin came back wearing black button boots, half way up her shin, the sort of thing that needed a buttonhook, Jean remembered, from the time she had played Eliza in a school production of *My Fair Lady*. No wonder it had taken a while to get them on. She had a lilac woolly knitted hat askew on her erratic hair. She reached for a pair of huge iron keys hanging on the hatstand, which had been within reach all the time, and Jean said, trying for Mark's sake to walk free with them, 'Please don't trouble yourself. You needn't bother to come. The School is unoccupied, isn't it?'

'In a way,' Miss Flewin said.

'Well, then . . . We'll bring them back as soon as

we're through with them. And you can stay indoors.'

'I am entrusted with them,' the old woman said. 'I would rather come.'

They found Mark prancing round the building. He had fetched a notebook and his camera from the car, and was writing things down, and taking snapshots. Miss Flewin walked so slowly that Jean could watch this going on while they approached like snails. And, she thought, we must be careful of this old woman, we must be patient, we must be kind, she may be our neighbour until she dies . . .

'When you get to be ninety,' her companion said, as though answering the unspoken thought, 'there's a lot of time for things. There has to be.'

The Schoolhouse door, framed by a little porch, was double. Once, long since, there had been two ways in, one marked 'Boys' the other marked 'Girls'. At some more rational period the door had been widened, made into a single, somewhat shapeless, wide archway, with the stone-cut labels left where they had always been, above it. The door creaked enthusiastically, as they went in. The Schoolhouse was a single, large room. Tall windows that didn't reach down enough to allow for looking out stood on its sunny side; it was open to the pitch of the roof, and wooden beams braced by iron rods painted green crossed the roofspace. At one end a pair of doors led through to a little lobby, with coathooks and lockers, and an old enamel sink. The one tap above it was lagged with strips of sacking. Lines of green mould ran down the walls, and a musty smell proclaimed the damp of ages.

But Mark was seized with delight. The cloakroom, he said, would be the kitchen, large, exquisitely fitted, opening into the main living space. That should certainly not be divided into boxes to make the usual number of rooms, all the wrong shape; instead they should build a gallery round three sides, leaving the main area open to

95

the roof, and put in a lovely Coalbrookdale iron stove on a tiled hearth.

'Where do we sleep?' Jean asked, trying to follow his flights of fancy.

'In the gallery.'

'Open to the living room?'

He smiled at her with a ghost of uncertainty in the smile. *Don't take this wrong*, his smile said. *Don't trip me up* . . . 'Dearest, if we ever do manage to get you in the family way, we can just put up some partition for the baby's room.' If they had been alone he would have put his arms round her, but any strangers made him stiff and remote . . .

'Of course,' she said. 'OK . . .'

'Hold the tape measure against that wall, will you?' he said. She stood, holding it, watching Miss Flewin, who had stepped into the cloakroom with them, reappear. Miss Flewin walked across an invisible grid in the floor. She was walking, Jean thought, round the desks that had once been there. She came slowly and stood quietly, hands folded, in front of the worn blackboard on the end wall. She was holding herself very straight, and gazing sternly and steadily at the vacant room.

She let the tape end drop and he wound it back, saying, 'Acres of space for everything!'

But Jean was staring at Miss Flewin. She could have sworn that the silent building was suddenly hushed, that Miss Flewin's glance had brought order, silence, a sense of expectation . . . she almost expected her next to rap the non-existent desk with a ruler, and announce morning prayers. And, she saw, completely certain, without the smallest scrap of a reason, that Miss Flewin did not just live in what had once been the school-mistress's cottage, she had been the schoolmistress. Mark was holding out the end of the tape to her again, to take the measurement the other way.

'Mark, look! What's that?' she said, pointing upwards.

A rope descended through a hole in the ceiling, looped sideways, and was hitched round a hook on the wall.

'The school bell!' Mark said, delighted. 'Don't you remember the pretty little lantern in the roof? The actual bell will have been taken down and sold, I expect.'

Miss Flewin smiled faintly. She made her way across the floor to the rope, taking again a curious right-angled route, as though her path were obstructed by things in rows. She unhooked the rope, and held the flocked end out to Jean, smiling faintly, interrogatively. Jean walked over to her, took the rope, and tugged it. For a moment she was back in the polished marble front hall of her own school, wearing her prefect's badge, feeling the resistance of her serge gymslip to her upward stretching arms. It was just the same now: for the first count, nothing . . . then a delayed loud bronze note. Recalling the way of it she tugged the rope with surprising energy, spacing the tugs. The notes rang late and regular, a fast imperious song.

Mark beamed. 'Oh, wonderful!' he said. 'We won't touch that. We'll find a way of ringing that from the new gallery level . . . how fantastic! Why, Jean, are you all right? Whatever is the matter?'

For Jean was drained of colour, and staring fixedly ahead. She was hearing things. As the last note of the bell died down, a tide of children's voices; children shouting, calling . . . a crowd of them, all over the vanished playground, their yelling and singing melded into a roar of sound, heard through each window, each wall . . . She thought at first it was a private madness, that her secret longing had finally tripped her reason; then she saw that Mark was frozen too, standing with the tape measure in his hands as though he were playing statues, and on Miss Flewin's face there was an expression of satisfaction. Head cocked, she was listening, smiling. The others were hearing it too. That joyful outburst, going on and on . . .

'You wouldn't think they would want to close a school with so many children round it,' Miss Flewin said, suddenly. 'They say there aren't enough children any more . . . I keep telling them, but they pay no heed. No heed of me at all.'

'But . . . where did they spring from?' said Mark, bewildered. 'Oughtn't they to be . . .?'

'At school?' said Miss Flewin. 'But of course they ought. They know that. But they don't know not to come here.'

Drifting through the window came a snatch of skipping song. Little girls' chirpy voices, singing:

Green gravel, green gravel, the grass is so green,
The fairest young lady that ever was seen!
Oh Liza, oh, Liza, your lover is dead!
And here comes a letter to turn round your head!

'They can tell the actual parents, of course,' Miss Flewin said. 'They can put letters in the post, telling them the school is closed, telling them to go to the one in Hampden, telling them about the school bus; but of course they can't tell these.'

'Ghosts?' said Mark, trying to laugh.

'Bless you, no, Mr Chittenden! Ghosts are the dead walking, aren't they? And these are not dead, oh, no.'

'But who are they?' asked Jean, a tremor running up and down her spine.

'I can tell if I listen,' the old lady said. 'That's John Thoroughgood shouting like that; and Tom Parsons answering him back. There's Grace and Netty Ramsey singing, and Ann Newbolt, and Bertie Hapgood counting skipping,—always plays with the girls, that one—and . . . but there. Names don't mean a thing to you. How could they?'

'And you remember them all?' said Mark, quietly.

'How could I ever forget them?' she said, 'when two of them are mine. Will they trouble you, do you think, Mrs Chittenden? I mean, if you take the school?'

'Children's voices?' Jean said. 'No. I like them.'

'Well then,' the old lady said. 'And you won't hear them often. I'll keep away. I'll keep my own side of that new fence. And you'll not often ring the bell for play.'

A unison chant sounded loud and clearly, above the other noise: 'The *wolf* has gone to *Devon*shire, and *won't* be back for *seven* year!'

'Good God!' said Mark. 'I haven't heard that since I was eight . . .'

Miss Flewin reached for the rope. She pulled three notes on the bell, and the voices ceased. They died down rapidly to whispers, shuffling of boots, complete silence . . . Straining her ears Jean heard once more the bird on the bush outside, and a car going along the road on the far side of the green . . .

'I knew the right people wouldn't mind,' Miss Flewin said, as she turned the iron key behind them in the door. 'There's been a lot of wrong people looking over it.'

They saw her to her gate, and took their leave of her, and walked away together across the green.

'Yes,' Jean said. 'Yes, this is it, love. Let's go and buy it.'

'You don't mind the neighbour being as mad as a bat?' he said. 'But, oh, just you wait, love! Just wait till you see what a house we can make of that! Such fun. We'll find an architect, but we'll keep him under control . . . I wonder where the old biddy keeps that tape-recorder; it had me shaken rigid for a bit.'

'They won't trouble us much, Mark,' she said. 'The voices, I mean. But they will be there sometimes. You'd better say now if you're going to mind them. They will be there sometimes, because I shall have Miss Flewin to tea now and then, and now and then I shall ring that bell.'

Their path back to the car led them across the green, past the war memorial, rather a florid one, with a bronze soldier, bayonet drawn, head bowed.

Mark stopped. 'My God, Jean,' he said. 'You can see why they put a stop to neighbourhood recruiting after the First World War. They seem to have lost half a regiment, all from this tiny place . . .'

But Jean was fixed in a silent stare again, staring at the long list of names and dates, the dates of young men who died just into adulthood, before anything had begun for them; and the names: Oliver Parsons, Ernest Thoroughgood, John Ramsey, Michael Newbolt, Percy Hapgood . . . What had Miss Flewin said? 'How could I forget them when two of them are mine . . .'

Suddenly Jean was crying, weeping again helplessly, her too frequent tears flowing now for the long forgotten defeat of natural hopes; not for the childless young men so much, quenched in the mud and chaos, nor even for the long solitudes they left to their girls behind them, but for the laughing and quarrelling and singing children who were not dead, having never been born.

The Tree and the Harp

GEORGE MACKAY BROWN

So, the dreadful old woman was dead at last. Old rich Mrs Maida was lying still and cold in her bed in the big house called The Hall.

The Hall stood down at the shore, an eighteenth-century house with a large garden surrounded by a high wall, so that Mrs Maida might have privacy from the coarse islanders.

One or two islanders there had to be inside the precincts, the two gardeners (one of whom, Sam, looked after the hives and the honey), and Miss Troll, the housekeeper who lived in the lodge—she had learned her trade in rich important houses in the south, and was even snootier than old Mrs Maida, though more prim —and Mrs Birsay, the cook and cleaner, and Mrs Birsay's girl Sophie, aged twelve. (Mrs Birsay was a widow.)

Sophie was glad that Mrs Maida was dead. She didn't exactly sing and dance; but she felt a shadow lifted from her. That terrible voice, that sarcasm that was like the flash and bite of a sword, would frighten Sophie no more!

At breakfast time her mother had come downstairs and whispered in the kitchen, 'She's dead! Poor Mrs Maida died in the night . . .' And then touched her eyes with the corner of her apron; for Mrs Birsay was a gentle-hearted woman. She had suffered greatly under Mrs Maida—no tyrant could have afflicted a loyal subject so horribly.

And Sophie wept to see her mother weeping. But inside, her heart was like a bird.

Only two weeks since that black voice had been ringing through the big house. 'Woman, this steak pie isn't fit to eat!' . . . 'You, woman, what d'you call yourself, Mrs Birsay, I nearly broke my teeth on the buns you baked this morning' . . . 'Birsay, you slut, there's a cobweb on the painting of my grandfather the general —there, woman, at the corner of the frame—clean it at once!' . . . 'No, I do *not* want a cup of tea. Say tea to me once more and I'll strangle you.'

And Sophie's mother had taken all these lies and insults and said nothing.

She knew her place, Sophie's mother.

Besides, if Mrs Maida had dismissed her, which she might well have done in one of her terrible tantrums, where could mother and daughter have gone?

There was no place in the world for them. Nowhere.

Sophie's father had been a sailor. They had lived in a rented house in the village. One winter, when Sophie was ten, a telegram had come—Bill Birsay had been lost at sea, swept overboard in a gale in Biscay.

They had had to be out of the house by November. After the grief, that was a gnawing worry. They had no relatives in the island. They were alone, and poor.

For many nights that summer Mrs Birsay and Sophie sat silent, looking into the fire, the tea growing cold in their cups.

Occasionally a man with a briefcase from the National Assistance office would come and ask tart questions.

One night there had come a prim knock on the cottage door. It was prim Miss Troll from the big house. 'It has come to Mrs Maida's notice that you might be available for general duties up at the Hall. Cooking and cleaning. Mrs Maida is very particular. She has a delicate stomach. She cannot bear untidiness in any shape or form. Please come to be interviewed at the Hall by Mrs Maida tomorrow morning at ten a.m. Should you prove acceptable, a room will be provided for you and the girl.'

And Mrs Birsay had gone to be interviewed—a harrowing experience—and she had been accepted. She was to start on Monday morning. Ten pounds a week, room and fire and food free; Wednesday afternoons off.

Mrs Birsay could have hugged Mrs Maida with gratitude. But one look from that basilisk eye quelled her.

'Thank you, ma'am,' murmured Mrs Birsay, and curtsied.

And so mother and daughter moved into the big house, at the beginning of spring.

And really, it was a nice little room on the ground floor they had, with a rosebush outside the window, and blackbirds singing from morning to night, and pigeons hopping and cooing round the kitchen door.

The garden was lovely. A little burn crept through it and out into the sea beyond the high wall. The burn, unfortunately, was sluggish and weed-choked and muted. Under the single tree it broadened into a dark deep pool, that looked sinister in the sunlight.

It would have been heaven for Sophie, if it hadn't been for the tyrant on the floor above. 'Listen, Mrs Birsay or whatever you call yourself, I can't eat soup with carrots or peas or onions in it. Please remember that!' . . . 'Woman, I didn't sleep a wink last night—you made the bed up all wrong' . . . 'Mrs Birsay, I don't want that girl of yours—what's her name, Sophie—wandering all over the garden. She'll ruin the flower-beds. *There's to be no climbing up that sycamore tree beside the pool*—I will *not* have your girl doing that' . . . 'Woman, come here at once—drop everything, a button has come off my blouse, sew it on' . . . 'How many times do I have to tell you, I only drink tea with my breakfast' . . . 'Do you ever think of anything but tea?'

So began this hideous tyranny that lasted for six months.

It had to be put up with. There was nothing else for it. Apart from the ten pounds a week, they were slaves.

How Sophie would have loved to wander through the forbidden garden! But if she set foot beyond the pavement that girdled the house one or other of the gardeners was there to shoo her away. They had been given their orders.

Even after the gardeners went home, at sunset, it was impossible. Mrs Maida was always on the watch from her high window, like a hawk.

But one night of full moon Sophie did it! Her mother was busy in the kitchen, preparing tomorrow's dinner. Miss Troll had gone to a church meeting. The tyrant had been in bed all day with a headache; her curtains were drawn.

Sophie looked; the curtains were still drawn. The moon had risen clear of the high garden wall. Beads of dew flashed from the flower-beds near and far, in the light of the full moon. And now the moon was looking through the sycamore leaves into the pool.

It was pure enchantment.

It was more than Sophie could bear.

She went like a shadow across the lawn. She stood under the tree. She seized the lowest branch and swung herself up into the tree. And the leaves whispered all about her.

Sophie looked down into the pool. It was dark and stagnant and sinister.

Then she heard a voice. 'Hello, I wish I had known you. Thirty years ago—thirty Julys—I sat in that tree. You're the first girl to sit in that fork of the tree since that night thirty summers ago. Welcome.'

Sophie was so startled she almost fell out of the tree. The voice had been sweet, distinct, beautiful.

Yet it was difficult to locate the music of the voice,

precisely. There was certainly no one to be seen, neither in the tree nor at the pool's edge nor among the bushes and flower-beds.

Sophie was on the point of dismissing the words as a part of the night's enchantment (for everything was lovely beyond words, really, and made perilous by the deep dark flashing pool below, and by the possibility that a dreadful eye was looking at her from the edge of a curtain.) Oh, she had never felt so moved and excited! She would tell nobody, not even her mother.

Now she *must* go in. She would be missed.

'I was a girl once, too.'

There was no mistaking the voice this time.

There was sadness in it, and loss, and pleading.

Sophie looked everywhere.

There was no girl to be seen.

Then the moon went behind a cloud.

Sophie dropped out of the tree. She moved across the garden like a shadow.

'Where have you been, Sophie? You look as if you'd seen a ghost. I'll put on a kettle for tea. Have you done your lessons? Oh, dear, I hope Mrs Maida will like this roast chicken, cold! I know it'll be good . . .'

Mrs Maida did not like the roast chicken. For five days she liked nothing that was offered to her.

She lay in bed, sipping barley water, with the blinds drawn, growling and complaining.

'Something, woman—surely there's *something* you can cook that'll lie on my stomach . . . That custard was like the yellow peril—take it away . . . Can't you even poach an egg, properly—I've had heartburn all day after that egg' . . . 'No, I do *not* want a nice cup of tea!'

If it wasn't the food, it was something else. 'This pillow's as hard as a stone' . . . 'I said I wanted a hot-water bottle, not a wishy-washy lukewarm thing' . . . 'That girl of yours, Sophie, makes far too much noise in the morning going to school—clack clack clack over the paving—can't you get her a pair of soft shoes?'

No doubt about it, the tyranny in the big house was growing blacker and heavier.

Even Miss Troll felt the lash of that tongue, and would pass up and down stairs with thin grey lips.

As for Mrs Birsay, nothing she did was right.

And Sophie knew that her mother was the very best cook and housekeeper in the island.

It was shameful, the way she was treated.

One had to make allowances for an invalid. But it was very difficult.

Now old Mrs Maida was more often in bed than out of it.

Dr MacIntyre called every day. Not even he was spared. 'Are you sure you're a proper doctor and not a quack? That last bottle you gave me nearly killed me. I want another prescription this time—something quite different. I sometimes think I'd be better with a tinker wife and her herbs.'

If, once or twice, Sophie came face to face with the dreadful old woman in the long corridor, she turned and fled! 'That's right, you little brat, off with you, get your mother to poison you with that awful tea she's forever making.'

But those chance encounters became fewer and fewer.

The old tyrant was getting weaker, no doubt about it.

Now, in late summer, she only got out of bed to shuffle on Miss Troll's arm to the garden chair between the rose bush and the fuchsia bush.

'Not there, you fool!' she wheezed one day when Miss Troll had set the garden chair for her under the sycamore tree, beside the pool. 'You ought to know better! Over there, beside the red roses . . .'

But, after five or ten minutes, it was, 'The bees are bothering me . . . There, I've got hayfever again—it's

that farmer cutting his hay. I could wring the fool's neck
. . . Take me inside.'

Illness had made her more dreadful in Sophie's eyes.
She glared here and there out of her grey shrunken mask
of a face.

And Miss Troll had to summon Mrs Birsay to help
carry the old rich wreck of a woman up to her bed.

Only twice in the month of August did Mrs Maida
venture into the beautiful garden—and then only
briefly. The butterflies revelled silently about her
departure, as she hobbled in on Miss Troll's arm.

And the two gardeners would light their pipes and
have a rest.

It was a large house of twenty rooms. For Sophie, it was
forbidden territory; she was confined to the bed-sitting
room and the kitchen.

'Oh,' her mother would cry, 'it's such a sad house! All
the rooms blinded, all the lovely furniture covered in
sheets. The loveliest room of all is the music room. Oh
Sophie, how I wish I could take you to the music room!
But I can't. Mrs Maida has forbidden it, strictly.'

(Mrs Birsay had to dust the deserted part of the house
twice a week.)

Sophie's curiosity, as harvest-time came and the farm-
folk cut their barley in the fields around, narrowed to the
music room. Sophie loved music, but—other than sing
—she had no chance to do anything about it. To play the
piano well was her greatest ambition. But that was out of
the question; there was no piano available, and fur-
thermore her mother couldn't afford to send her to the
lady in the village who gave piano tuition.

As the darker nights of autumn drew in, Mrs Birsay
spent most of her time sewing and knitting. Now the
mistress of the big house could take only the lightest of
food: fruit juices, poached fish, beaten-up eggs. So Mrs
Birsay justified her existence by knitting bedsocks for the

107

invalid, and making curtains of the old rich materials she had found in a chest in the attic; so that it might cheer up the invalid.

But all she did was grumble. Nothing was right. Her voice had lost its black edge. It was old and grey and hopeless now.

'What do I want fine curtains for? They should have been hung thirty years ago . . . What did you say the name of your girl was? Sophie? Tell Sophie she can sing if she wants to—she has a nice voice. I heard her the other evening, singing under my window . . . No tea, not even for breakfast—it tastes of nothing . . . Nothing tastes of anything any more . . . I feel very tired . . . Tell that Troll woman not to come near me. She looks more and more like an undertaker or a gravedigger . . . The curtains are quite pretty, Mrs Birsay, but they're thirty years too late . . . Tell Sophie she is *not to go into the garden* . . .'

It was pathetic, Mrs Birsay told Sophie, to see how weak and shrunken the old lady had become.

'I think,' said Mrs Birsay, 'she'll never be out of that bed again . . .'

Why did those words put a sudden glitter in Sophie's eyes?

The big house was quiet after tea.

Miss Troll had gone to visit another spinster who lived at the far end of the island, on WRI business.

Mrs Birsay was sewing cushion covers out of the roll of material she had discovered in the attic. The mistress had said she could do anything she liked with it. Mrs Maida, once her health began to improve, might enjoy bright cushions in the rooms, instead of the old sun-faded ones. So Mrs Birsay sewed and hemmed and drank endless cups of tea.

The old invalid was presumably drowsing in her bed. More and more she was lost under the tides of sleep.

Sophie, without a word, slipped out of the room, and

began to explore the house. She carried a candle with a yellow flower of flame floating above.

Where was the music room?

Oh, it was eerie! Sophie opened room after room —each, in the candle-light, was an immense silent theatre of shadows. The shadows crowded about her. All the chairs and tables were covered, as if they were dead and waiting for the worms. Sophie shut door after door. Her thudding heart must be the loudest thing in the house.

Once a drop of hot candle wax fell on her hand! She almost screamed.

She opened a door. Another dance of shadows, a silent gathering. Ah, but this must be the music room. That shrouded shape over there could only be the piano! Sophie moved over towards the piano. Her glimmer of light discovered a white bust on the mantelshelf, with the name 'Chopin' on the base—and over there, against the wall, a Celtic harp. Sophie touched a string—it gave out a rich pure note—the whole house seemed to echo the golden sound.

A voice said, 'Oh, if I had known you thirty years ago! . . . We would have had such happy times . . . Yes, I'd have taught you to play the harp, and the piano too . . . I think I'd have had no better friend than you . . . Too late, too late . . .'

The voice was clear and unmistakable; it was the voice she had heard in the garden.

This time, there was no enchantment of moonlight to shake it out of nothingness; only a feeble candle-flame, and a harp stroke.

Sophie was not in the least afraid: there was such an air of welcome in the music room, though it was tinged by sadness and regret a little.

The reverberations of the harp stroke seemed to go on for a long time. Then the room was stark and cold again.

Sophie stayed there as long as she dared.

She *must* go back—she would be missed. (She ought to have been bent over her homework.)

She descended the wide stair, softly, led by the yellow petal of flame.

Coming round the corner into the long corridor that ended in the kitchen, Sophie almost ran into a frail figure lingering at the foot of the great stairway.

The girl cried out with terror! It was Mrs Maida. The candle fell on the floor and went out.

The old woman put leaf-light hands on Sophie's shoulder. 'Sunniva, I heard you at the harp, dear,' she said. 'It was lovely, I thought there would never be music in this house, ever again . . . Oh, I know it's lonely for you here in this big house, I know it is. I can't think what to do about that, Sunniva. You can't mix with the village girls. That's out of the question. I know you'd like to speak to them, maybe invite a girl or two up to the house. I'll think about it. Maybe some day. It's hard to know what to do for the best . . . If only your parents were still alive . . . Yes, dear, you can walk in the garden if you like. It's such a lovely night. Then supper and bed. What, you'd like to climb up into that tree? I don't see why not. You're light and strong enough . . .'

What was the old woman talking about?

'I'm Sophie,' said the girl. 'I'm sorry for wandering about the house like this. I didn't do any harm.'

'Come and kiss me goodnight once you're in from the garden, Sunniva,' said Mrs Maida in a gentle voice.

Then she put her twisted hand on the banister and began slowly to climb the stair to her room.

That night, she died.

Miss Troll came into her own, briefly, making arrangements for the funeral. Only the gentry were invited, of course, and the village merchant and the farmer from the big farm and the local councillor and Dr MacIntyre. As things turned out, very few attended the funeral in the little family burial-place next to the Hall. The weather was bad. And nobody had liked the dead woman very much.

Miss Troll had done the things that ought to be done at a funeral. There was sherry for the mourners, and plates of smoked salmon on toast, and little cakes that Mrs Birsay had made. The few mourners lingered awhile in the drawing-room, made a few valedictory remarks, then went away with their long insincere faces.

Miss Troll permitted herself a thin smile as the last of them went. She had done her duty.

Neither Mrs Birsay nor Sophie had been invited to the funeral, of course.

Mrs Birsay had the longest face of all, not only that day but for several days to come. From time to time she touched her eyes with the corner of her apron. The kettle was always on the boil. The teapot was never empty.

What would become of her and Sophie now? Once more they would be out in the cold winds.

'You may stay where you are meantime,' said Miss Troll. 'Mrs Maida was the last of the family. No doubt the house will be sold. The family lawyers in Edinburgh have the disposing of the estate. We will just carry on as we're doing until we receive official notice. No doubt my services to Mrs Maida, extending over forty years, will not be forgotten.'

This last sentence was spoken with a tinge of anxiety. It was obvious that Miss Troll was not at all sure as to how things would fall out. If she had been, she would not have spoken the way she did to a mere servant like Mrs Birsay. It was the first time Miss Troll had ever visited the Birsays' room.

As the days passed, anxiety began to eat into her more and more. She took to visiting Mrs Birsay twice or thrice a day in the kitchen. (Mrs Birsay was a good listener.) She even condescended to drink cups of tea.

'I was very faithful to Mrs Maida,' she said, permitting

Sophie's mother to pour her yet another cup of tea. 'I might go so far as to say, I sacrificed my prospects for her. For, after the terrible thing happened, she was almost out of her mind. Had I not been there, to support her, who knows what she might not have done? I was a rock of strength to her, when she needed me most. And I devoted all the rest of my days to her. I'm sure she won't have forgotten me in her will. But did she ever *make* a will? She didn't like talk of death and wills and tombstones—she couldn't stand the thought of her latter end. The lawyers in Edinburgh, they must know what I've sacrificed for Mrs Maida.'

So that was it—the prim proud spinster was even more terrified than Mrs Birsay as to what might become of her, now that the earth had closed over the mistress of the house.

She had lived for forty years in the lodge at the end of the drive: it was a part of her; it was unthinkable that ever she might have to leave it.

'There are no immediate relatives,' said Miss Troll. 'There are, I think, some distant cousins in Canada and South Africa. They were little help to her when the tragedy happened. They never even wrote a letter of sympathy. In fact, I doubt if Mrs Maida had even *seen* them all her life long. How awful, if they were to inherit the estate!'

'Well,' said Mrs Birsay, 'it must have been a sad thing for her indeed, losing her husband.'

'Pooh!' said Miss Troll. 'She never shed a tear for *him*. Mr Maida had his own house, in Perthshire. I quite liked Mr Maida, he was always civil to me. Then suddenly he left, without so much as a goodbye. Mind you, Mrs Maida could sometimes be a difficult person to live with. Between you and me, but for Charles, their son, he'd have left her much sooner. As soon as Charles was found a suitable position in the city, and settled, Mr Maida was up and off.'

'A son!' cried Mrs Birsay. 'So there's a son!'

'There *was* a son,' said Miss Troll. 'He was killed in a car crash in Yorkshire, himself and his wife, two years after they were married. They were on their way north, for a holiday, with the baby, to see her.'

'That was a terrible thing to happen!' said Mrs Birsay. 'No wonder she had her dark moods from time to time.'

'She didn't roll a tear down her cheek for that either,' said Miss Troll. 'Not one single tear, that ever I saw. She was like one of those ancient Roman matrons you read about—all strength and resolution.'

'And the baby, it was killed too?' sighed Mrs Birsay.

'Oh, no. The child survived . . . "What home or institution will I place the creature in?" Mrs Maida said twenty times if she said it once in the course of the next few days, while the funeral arrangements were going on. (Mr and Mrs Charles are buried out there too, in the same place as the mistress.) "I can't have a brat about here," she declared. "I couldn't put up with it for an hour" . . . Then suddenly, on the evening of the double funeral, she rounded on me and she declared, "Troll, I think I'd better have this grandchild here. I'll give it a try, anyway" . . .'

'The poor child!' said Mrs Birsay—and at once she could have bit out her tongue for saying it.

'Not poor child in the slightest,' said Miss Troll. 'I never in my life beheld such a beautiful happy child, right from the start. And that same child caused a miracle in this house. The streams ran, the desert blossomed as a rose. That same child, I assure you, gave Mrs Maida twelve years of the most wonderful happiness! It was a blessing in her life. This house seemed to be overflowing with music and laughter all the time . . . Ah, she played the piano like an angel, Sunniva. Alas!'

'What happened?' whispered Mrs Birsay, and brought the corner of her apron up to her eyes again.

'You see that tree out there in the garden?' said Miss

113

Troll. 'Over there by the pool. One summer evening Sunniva—that was her name—climbed up into the tree. A branch broke. She fell into the pool and was drowned. Nobody saw it. The gardeners lifted her body out of the pool next morning, and carried it into the house. "Lay her in the music room," said Mrs Maida coldly . . .'

Mrs Birsay choked on her sobs; beyond speech she was.

'From that day,' said Miss Troll, 'winter and night descended on this house. I thought, for a month and more afterwards, that she would go mad. Dr MacIntyre shook his head. "It's more than you or I can handle, Miss Troll," he said. "If she could weep," he said, "she might improve. As things are, she'll will herself into the grave. What's the name of that old Greek sculptor whose statues seemed to have the breath of life in them?—Here we have the opposite process, a living woman turning herself to stone in front of our eyes. I can't do a thing about it . . ." For a month she did not speak. She hardly moved. I think, though, she cried in secret. I would see her, morning after morning, with the stains on her face. Then one morning she spoke. "Troll," she said, "I want all the rooms closed up. Cover the furniture. Draw the blinds. Stop the clocks. Only the few needful rooms are to be used . . ." So, in a way, she recovered. But the terrible scar was in her mind and heart and spirit to her dying day . . . Not that she ever mentioned Sunniva. One day, some time later, I happened to say, "That sycamore, it might be better cut down, don't you think? And the pool is stagnant—it ought to be drained?" . . . Oh, Mrs Birsay, I have never before or since endured such a storm of rage! The tree and the pool would stand till they rotted! I was never to mention such a thing again . . . Poor silly me, I never know when enough is enough. I suppose it might have been a year later that I said, "Mrs Maida, the girl Seenie," (Seenie used to come twice a week to dust and polish) "Seenie," I said, "tells me one of the harp-strings is broken in the music room. Will I have it seen to?'' Such a sudden blaze of anger! ''Nobody is to touch a thing in the music room, now or at any other time. Never so much as mention music room again, you withered old witch!'' So, Mrs Birsay, I learned my lesson the hard way. Many a time I was sorely tempted to leave her. But time passed, and I grew older, and at last I knew I would stay with her till the end.'

'I have never heard anything so sad!' sighed Mrs Birsay. 'Poor Mrs Maida—I forgive her the one or two hard things she said to me.'

'It's come at last,' said Miss Troll, producing a letter from her handbag. 'A solicitor from the firm in Edinburgh is coming on Monday. For some reason, he wants to see you and Sophie also. I suppose it's a good sign that the letter's addressed to me . . . No, thank you, Mrs Birsay, I won't have any more tea.'

Miss Troll's hand trembled as she put the letter back into her handbag.

Sophie raced through the big house, room after room, pulling up blinds, tearing the covers from chairs, tables, sideboards, throwing open the windows so that, after thirty years' stagnation, the air could flow in.

She was behaving like a crazy girl.

Sometimes she laughed. Sometimes she cried. She had to sit down, from time to time, for a little rest. But never for long. It was out into the corridor with her, into another room: the blinds jerked up, window sash opened, covers whisked off. Beautiful hidden objects declared themselves: clocks, bookcases, bowls and jars of great beauty, tapestried chairs, portraits in gilt frames, round oak tables.

And they were all hers!

Sophie threw open a high drawing-room window. The two gardeners, Sam and Willie, were idling below— since Mrs Maida's death they had turned noticeably lazier. 'Hey, you two!' shouted Sophie. 'I want that pool under the tree cleaned out at once. Do you hear me? I want the burn to go singing into it and out the other side, like it used to do. Get started!'

Sam and Willie turned astonished faces up at her.

'Your wages are to be increased by five pounds a week,' cried Sophie.

Then she ran along the corridor to another room that had been in silent mourning for thirty years, and let the air and the light in, and set free the lovely furniture, pictures, ornaments. She adjusted the weights in the tall bronze clock. The pendulum swung—time began again in the room.

She had to sit down and have a longer rest. The wonder of all that happened that day had exhausted her.

An hour ago the Edinburgh lawyer had left the house, having read the will.

It was the strangest will ever read.

The memory of Miss Troll's face, at the part that concerned her, sent Sophie into another wild outburst of merriment . . . 'To Martha Troll, my companion, I leave and bequeath one pot of honey a month, in the vain hope that it may sweeten her disposition.'

Sophie had never seen anything so droll as the look on Miss Troll's face then! The girl rocked back and fore in the chair with laughter. She laughed till tears streamed down her cheeks.

Delight and wonderment echoed in room after room. It was hers—all hers!

The look on her mother's face had been almost as comical. 'To my cook and cleaning-woman, Mrs Sandra Birsay, as her existence seems to be devoted mainly to the brewing of tea, I leave my best china teapot, along with half-a-dozen matching cups and saucers, so that she can make tea everlasting from this day to the day of her funeral.'

'That lovely teapot mine!' Mrs Birsay had cried. 'How kind!'

As for Miss Troll, after the first horrified gape at the lawyer's mouth pronouncing sentence, an extraordinary sequence of expressions had passed across her face: bewilderment, rage, disbelief, self-pity, sorrow, resignation, despair.

Sophie, going between two rooms, cried over the banister, so that the two women drinking tea in the kitchen could hear her, 'Don't worry, Miss Troll! The gatehouse is yours—I'm giving it to you. You are to have fifty pounds a week pension from today on.'

The next room that Sophie went into was the music room . . . How beautiful it looked with the sun shining in and the rosewood piano uncovered for the first time. It was locked. Sophie found the key on the mantelpiece, under the portrait of a beautiful young woman who bore a striking resemblance to Mrs Maida as she might have looked sixty years before . . . Sophie's hand moved at random over the keyboard—ah, now she would be able to have lessons; she could well afford it! The notes roused echoes all over the upper storey of the big house. There were music sheets in the piano stool, with the name 'Sunniva Maida' written in a round immature script.

Sophie kissed the plaster cheek of Chopin.

Two hundred and fifty thousand, five hundred and twenty-one pounds and three pence . . . That's how much Sophie was worth, since an hour ago. 'As well as the Hall and all the grounds and outhouses, and furnishings and objects of art and all appurtenances whatsoever belonging to the Hall, I leave and bequeath the residue of my estate to the girl Sophie Birsay: in the fair hope that, after such a long winter, she will bring April into a dead house and, after April, a long long summer filled with song, blossom, and the laughter of children, for many generations.'

The voice of the little lawyer, unused to such poetry in

the documents he handled, had paused to say, 'The late Mrs Maida's own words . . . The residue of the estate, after the deduction of all taxes, duties, fees, and expenses, amounts to £250,521:03. In due course, a cheque for that amount will be sent to the young lady I see sitting before me.'

He had given Sophie a thin conspiratorial smile.

Poor Miss Troll still sat, petrified by the thunderbolt. Her mother had managed to say, 'A cup of tea will do us all the world of good.'

A teapot and six cups and saucers! Sophie leaned over the banister rail. 'Mother, I will get a golden teapot specially for you. I appoint you housekeeper here in the Hall. Your salary will be one hundred pounds a week . . .'

Whispers down below, in the kitchen, and the clink of cups. More tea had been brewed, obviously. There would be an ocean of tea in that kitchen before nightfall!

Sophie found herself in the room of death before she was aware of it. Here Mrs Maida had endured the last thirty years of her life. Here, three weeks ago, she had died.

Sophie threw open the window. The gardeners, Sam and Willie, were already beginning to clear the choked burn. She could actually hear the first singing of the waters. Soon there would be a little blue lake under the sycamore tree, reflecting the birds and leaves of summer.

Sophie opened a cupboard and found bundles of letters tied with red ribbons. Someone, far back in time, had loved Mrs Maida.

Ah, the excitement of the day had wrung Sophie dry! As she went down the wide stairway—*her* stairway, in *her* vast house—to get a cup of tea before the teapot was dry, she heard the music from the music room: wistful, delicate, heartbreaking, yet it trembled (lingering) on the verge of an all-but-impossible promise.

The Tower

AIDAN CHAMBERS

'Surely you understand now,' Mr Phelps said, patient and smiling. 'I've explained it to you three times, Martin.'

His son sighed and stared at the Ordnance Survey map spread out on the caravan table.

'I know,' he said. 'It's just that I'm sure there was a tower exactly where I've marked it.'

'You've got it wrong, nitwit. I keep telling you, there's a pond there, that's all.' The smile had gone now.

'I suppose.'

'What do you mean, you suppose!'

'But the map could be wrong. Or you could be wrong yourself.'

Mr Phelps drew in his breath. 'Martin, there are times when I wonder if you have any brains at all. I've told you—I've seen it. The map is accurate and *I am not wrong!*'

'Don?' Mrs Phelps was lying face down on a travelling rug spread on the grass just outside the caravan door. 'Remember, dear, we're on holiday.' Though pretending to sleep as she sunbathed in her bikini, she had been eavesdropping on the conversation, half expecting it to end in a row.

Mr Phelps shuffled from his seat behind the table and went to the door, his walking boots clumping on the floor and his angry weight making the caravan tremble.

'Well,' he chuntered, 'he really is stupid as well as stubborn sometimes, Mary. I've explained till I'm blue in the face but he just doesn't seem capable of taking it in.'

'Maybe he has a blind spot for maps.'

'A blind spot for maps! Mary, you can't have a blind spot for maps. You can, perhaps, for French or maths. But not for *maps*. They're designed so any fool can understand.'

He stared across the heat-hazed field to the woods beyond and wondered why he hadn't gone off on his walk alone instead of listening to his son blathering about a tower that wasn't there and the map being wrong.

Mrs Phelps flopped on to her back, put her sunglasses on and patted the rug at her side.

'Come and sit here for a few minutes,' she said.

Her husband obeyed, squatting cross-legged, his arms hugging his knees.

'I wouldn't mind,' he said, more in regret than anger now, 'if he just listened a bit more carefully. But he argues. Doesn't try to learn first.'

'It's his age,' Mrs Phelps said. 'I bet you were just the same when you were fourteen.'

'Never!'

His wife laughed, gently. ''Course you were, everybody is.'

'Not me. I was keen to know about things. Everything. Information, that's what it's about. You don't get to know things by arguing the toss with someone who knows more than you do. You listen. Question. Pick their brains.'

Mrs Phelps stroked her husband's knee. 'Well, you aren't in school now. Just relax. Enjoy yourself. That's what holidays are for.'

Mr Phelps edged his legs out of range of his wife's hand.

The summer afternoon sang.

'Maybe,' Mrs Phelps said after a while, but quietly so that Martin wouldn't hear, 'maybe we should have let him go off with his friends after all.'

'Camping with a bunch of yobs? Not on!'

'You're too hard on him.'

'He'll appreciate it later.'

'At his age you need some freedom, Don. A life of your own.'

'Ho!' Mr Phelps snorted. 'Freedom to act like an idiot, you mean. Freedom to roam the streets and vandalize bus shelters. Freedom to terrorize old people and mess yourself up with drugs. Some freedom that is!'

'What makes you think Martin would behave like that?'

'Oh, come on, Mary. You've seen the rubbish who hang around our place. I passed a gang of them the other night. Half of them smoking their heads off while they watched the other half make a meal of the local females. About which enough said!'

Mrs Phelps sighed. 'That's a kind of learning too, I suppose.'

Her husband flicked a hand at a bombarding fly. 'Well, as far as I'm concerned, it's a lesson Martin can do without, thanks.'

For a few moments neither spoke.

Mr Phelps whisked at more attacking flies, but with less ferocity now.

'Why not go for your walk?' Mrs Phelps said when she was sure the storm had blown over.

Her husband stood up in one smooth movement without using his hands. 'Perhaps I will.' He tucked his shirt in and hitched his trousers. 'There's a long barrow just north of us. No record of it being excavated. I'll poke about there for a while. Might be interesting.'

He collected his stick from the back of the car, said, 'See you in a couple of hours,' and stalked away.

*

From his seat in the caravan Martin watched his father stride across the field, climb the gate in the hedge and disappear up the lane. Then he returned his gaze to the map lying on the table at his elbows. A week ago he had been looking at it with excited anticipation. Now he regarded it with distaste. Nothing ever turned out as well as you hoped.

He slipped out from behind the table, took an apple from the basket in the food cupboard, bit into its juicy crispness, went to the door and sat on the step, his feet square on the ground.

The noise of his munching was loud in the country silence.

'Enjoying it?' his mother said.

Martin nodded, knowing she was watching from behind her dark glasses.

'He'll feel better after his walk,' Mrs Phelps said.

Martin nodded again.

He gnawed his apple to the core, then lobbed it high over his mother's body to fall in the long grass beyond. From where it landed a small dark bird he couldn't recognize flew up, startled. If his father had still been here, he would have insisted on him looking it up in his recognition book.

'Could I help?' Mrs Phelps asked.

'Doubt it,' Martin said, squinting as he tried to follow the bird's flight into the sun.

Mrs Phelps sat up and swivelled to face him. 'Won't you tell me what the trouble is?'

'Doesn't matter.'

'You were having quite a set-to for something that doesn't matter.'

Martin shrugged. 'It's just that I say the map is wrong, and Dad says I don't know how to read it properly.'

Mrs Phelps took her sunglasses off. 'What do you say is wrong?'

Martin sighed. 'You know how he set me a route to walk this morning to prove I could use the map on my own?'

'Yes.'

'Well, I managed all right really. Just missed a couple of details. Only little things. But on the last leg down Tinkley Lane . . .'

'The one that runs along the far side of this field?'

'Yes. There's a quarry along there, about a mile away, and a bench mark, and a couple of disused farm buildings, and I got them all OK . . .'

'But?'

'In a field with a pond in it about three quarters of a mile away—eight tenths, actually, to be exact—I saw a tower.'

'And?'

'It isn't marked on the map so I put it in.'

'But Dad says it isn't there?'

Martin nodded.

Mrs Phelps put her sunglasses on again. 'But, sweetheart, I don't see the problem. Either the tower is there or it isn't.'

'That's what we were rowing about.'

Mrs Phelps laughed. 'Men! Why row? Why not just go and find out together?'

'I wanted to. But Dad wouldn't.' Martin stood up. 'He said he knew it wasn't there. He said he'd been along that way twice already since we got here and he'd never seen a tower. But I know it is there, Mum, I saw it this morning, certain sure.'

'All right, all right!' Agitation in her son's voice warned that care was needed. 'Come here. Sit down. Let's have that shirt off. Get some sunlight on you. You're as bad as your dad. You both think you'll evaporate if you get sun on your body.'

Reluctantly, Martin tugged his shirt off and sat so

that his mother could rub sun oil on to his back.

'This tower,' she said as she anointed him, 'what did it look like?'

'A bit weird really. Built of stone and quite high. Fifteen metres. Twenty maybe. And it was round. With little slit windows, with pointed tops like in a church. But there wasn't a spire or anything, it was just flat, with battlements round the top like a castle. There was a biggish doorway at the bottom, with an arch like the windows. But there was no door. And the wall was partly covered in ivy, and weeds and even clumps of flowers were growing out of the cracks between some of the stones.'

'How exciting. Lie down and I'll do your front.'

'No, I'll do myself.'

Martin took the tube and began oiling his chest.

'Did you go inside?'

'I started pacing towards it because I wanted to try and fix its position on the map exactly. But after thirty paces, well before I even reached the pond . . . I don't know . . . the air went chilly. Just all of a sudden. Like I'd come up against a wall of cold.'

He stopped rubbing the oil and looked at his mother's masked eyes.

'Made me feel a bit scared. Don't know why. There weren't any cattle in the field, nothing to be scared of, you know. But I stopped pacing and just stood. And then I noticed how quiet the place was. I mean quiet in an odd sort of way.'

Martin paused, his eyes now not focused, though he was looking straight at his mother.

'And what was so odd?' Mrs Phelps said as calmly as she could.

Martin's eyes focused again.

'No birds,' he said. 'None flying anywhere near and not a sound of any birdsong either. Not even insects. Nothing. Just dead silence.'

Mother and son stared at each other.

'Perhaps a kestrel lives in the tower? Or some other bird of prey?'

Martin shook his head.

'You can't be sure.'

'Can.'

'How?'

'Went in.'

'Even though you were scared?'

'I'm trying to tell you!'

'All right, OK, I'm listening.'

'It was pretty hot this morning, right?'

His mother nodded.

'A heat haze, just like now?'

'Was there?'

'I didn't notice either till I was in the field looking at the tower. I'd noticed about the birds and was looking at the tower. It seemed normal, just an old stone building, you know. The field all around is long grass, like this one, with a tall hedge, and a wood opposite from the lane side. And it was while I was looking at the wood that it hit me.'

He stopped, uncertain of himself.

'Go on, sweetheart,' Mrs Phelps said.

'Well, everything, the wood and the hedge and the grass in the field, even the pond—everything was shimmering in the haze. But the tower . . . It wasn't. It was quite still. The shape of it was clear cut.'

Mrs Phelps gave an involuntary shudder. She didn't really believe Martin's story. Not that he would lie. He never lied. But he did get carried away by his imagination sometimes. Even so—a tower standing cold and silent in the middle of a summer field. She shuddered again. Curious how a few words, just by association, can make you feel cold on a lovely day in hot sunshine.

She came back to herself. Martin was still telling his story and she had missed something. She said, 'Sorry, lovey, I was distracted. What did you say?'

'The tower,' Martin said. 'It was cool inside, wonderfully cool, and restful.'

'Wasn't it locked up?'

'No, I told you, I went straight in. There was a doorway but no door. And inside the place was smelly, really stank, like empty places often do, don't they, as if people have used them for lavatories. But it was quite clean, no rubbish or anything. A round-shaped room with a bare earth floor. And one of the little pointed windows with no glass in it. And a stone stairway, that started just inside the door and curled up round the wall to a floor above. No banister, just the stone stairs in the wall.'

'No sign of life?'

'Nothing. Deserted. And very cool. Really nice after the heat. Well, anyway, I thought it must have a smashing view from the top, so I climbed the stairs. Thirty-two. Counted them. Eighteen to the first floor, and fourteen to the top. The first floor was just old wooden boards. A few bird droppings but nothing else.'

'And safe. Not rotten or anything?'

'No. I wouldn't have gone on if it hadn't been safe, would I? I'm not that stupid, whatever Dad thinks!'

'It's just his manner. So was there a good view?'

'Not really. After the field there's trees in the way in most directions. But it was nice. There's a parapet so you can't fall off. And it was just as cool up there as inside. I'd have stayed longer, but I knew if I didn't get home in reasonable time, Dad would start getting at me for taking so long to do a simple route. So I came down, paced the distance back to the lane, marked the position on the map, and came back.'

Mrs Phelps took a deep breath. 'What a story!'

Martin glared at her. 'It is *not* a story. It's what happened.'

His mother leaned to him and hugged his face to hers. 'Yes, my love, I know,' she said. 'I mean, what a strange thing to find a tower like that and it not be on the map.'

Martin pulled free. 'Don't you start!'

Mrs Phelps leaned back on her hands. 'Did you tell your father all this?'

Martin grimaced in disdain.

'No,' his mother said. 'Best not to, I suppose.'

'He wouldn't believe me about the tower being there. So you know what he'd say about the rest. Rubbish, he'd say, pure imagination.'

Mrs Phelps thought for a while then stood up and adjusted her bikini. 'Look, why don't I slip into something respectable and you can show me your tower? That'll settle matters.'

Martin shook his head.

'Why not? If I've seen it he can't go on saying it isn't there.'

'But that'll only make it worse. He'll get angry and say we ganged up against him, that I got you to take my side, that I can't stand on my own feet.'

Impasse.

After a sullen moment Mrs Phelps said, 'I'll tell you what. You go on your own, and double-check the position of the tower. After all, you just might have made a mistake. Then come back and tell me. After supper this evening, I'll suggest we take a walk, and I'll make sure we go along Tinkley Lane past the tower. That way, we'll all see it together and your father won't be able to say you're wrong. How about that?'

Martin considered.

'OK,' he said, cheering up. 'But I know it's where I said it was.'

''Course it is, my love. But make sure. And while you're gone I'll fix supper so that everything's ready when your father gets back.'

Martin pulled on his shirt, collected his map from the caravan, folded it so he could hold it easily and see the area round the tower, gave his mother a tentative hug, and set off across the field.

Mrs Phelps watched her son out of sight before going

inside, pulling on a pair of jeans and an old shirt of her husband's, and slipping her feet into her sandals.

Martin sauntered down the lane, stifled by the heat cocooned between the high, dense hedgerows. Wasps and flies whirred past his head. A yellow-hammer pink-pinked behind him. Straight above, crawling across the dazzling blue, a speck of aeroplane spun its white spider thread.

His shirt clung uncomfortably to his oiled body. He glanced up the lane and down, and, seeing no one, tugged his shirt off and used it as a fly-whisk as he walked along. Usually he kept himself covered, too embarrassed by his scrawny build to show himself in public. Boys at school called him Needle.

Even without his shirt he was sweating by the time he reached the gateless opening in the hedge that led to the tower. And sure enough, there it was, looking just as it had in the morning. This time he noticed at once how coldly it stood and clearly outlined while all around grass and flowers and trees and rocks and even the pond at the foot of the tower shimmered in the haze. And while he looked, just as that morning, he felt a nerve-tingling strangeness. He tried to work out what the strangeness was and decided it was like knowing something was going to happen to you but not quite knowing what.

There must, Martin thought, be some ordinary explanation. His father would probably know what it was, and would tell him, if only he would stop insisting that the tower wasn't there, and come and see for himself while the heat haze was still rising. By this evening, when his mother tricked his father into seeing the tower, the haze would have vanished into a dew.

As he checked its position on his map, Martin remembered the coolness and how much he had wanted to stay in the tower. Now there was nothing to hurry back to the caravan for. He could stay and enjoy himself. He might even make a den, a secret place where he could come and be by himself during the rest of the week. Nor had he properly explored the building; there was bound to be something interesting if he looked carefully enough. There was also the pond; there might be fish to be caught. And if he wanted to sunbathe, the tower roof was a good place; no one could see him lying behind the parapet, but he would be able to spy anyone approaching across the field. He might even go home after the holiday with a useful tan.

He was about to enter the field when he heard a shout. A cry, in fact, rather than a yell. A girl's voice, high-pitched and desperate. Coming from the direction of the tower.

Shading his eyes with a hand, he searched the tower but could see no one.

The cry came again. And suddenly he knew what caused the strangeness he felt. It was as if he had been waiting for this cry, that it had reached him as a sensation long before he heard it as a sound in his ears.

As he stared at the tower with fixed unblinking eyes, he saw a girl's head, then her body appear above the parapet till she was revealed to her waist. She was about fifteen or sixteen and wearing a sleeveless white summer-loose dress. But from this distance it was difficult to see her features clearly, which anyway were partly hidden by long dark hair that fell around her shoulders.

She grasped the wall of the parapet with one hand. The other she raised above her head and waved urgently at Martin. At first he thought she was only excited, perhaps pretending to be frightened by the height. But then she cried out again in that high-pitched urgent voice.

She seemed to be shouting, 'Come back, come back!' and waving him towards her.

But that could not be. He had never seen her before.

Puzzled, Martin did not move, except to raise his own

hand and wave back in a polite reflex action.

Still the girl waved and cried, 'Come back, come back!'

She's mistaken me for someone else, Martin thought. But even as he thought this, smoke began to drift up from the tower behind the girl, first only a thin blue smudge in the air, which quickly became a thicker feathering, and then, after a belching puff, a dense, curling ribbon that streamed straight up into the sky, grey-white against the deep blue.

As the smoke thickened, the girl's cries became more panic-stricken, her hand-waving more frantic.

Which at last brought Martin to life again. Dropping his shirt and map, he sprinted towards the tower.

Mrs Phelps gave her son a few minutes' start before setting off after him. But she got no further than the gate when she met her husband striding down the lane towards her. She knew at once that he was excited from the jaunty way he was windmilling his stick.

'You'll never guess,' he said as he approached.

'What?' Mrs Phelps grinned, expecting some story about her husband finding an almost extinct flower or spotting a rare bird.

'Just been talking to an old farmer. Asked him if he knew of a stone tower anywhere in the district . . .' He paused, enjoying the drama.

'And?'

'At first he said no. Nothing of that sort round here, sir!' Mr Phelps, who prided himself on his talent for mimicry, imitated the farmer's accent. 'Then he remembered. Ah, wait a minute, sir, he says, yes there were one. But that were years back, sir, when I were a boy, like.'

Mrs Phelps caught at her breath.

Her husband went on, unaware. 'I quizzed him——without letting on about Martin, of course. Apparently, there used to be an old teasel tower where the pond is just down the lane from here. You know the sort. You always say they look as if they're straight out of a fairy tale. Sleeping Beauty, Rapunzel and all that rubbish. And we came across a teasel growing wild just the other day, remember? Rather like a tall thistle, with a large very prickly head. Well, it was the heads they dried in those towers and then used them for raising the nap on cloth. Fascinating process . . .'

'Yes, darling, but . . .?'

'. . . They cut the dried heads in two and attached them to a cylinder which revolved against the cloth in such a way that the prickles snagged against the fabric just sufficiently to scuff the surface.' Mr Phelps chuckled. 'Teasing it, you might say!'

'Don . . .'

'And do you know, Mary, they still haven't been able to invent a machine that can do the job better. Isn't that extraordinary!'

'Don, the tower—what did the old man tell you?'

'I'm just coming to that. According to the old chap, one day during a long hot summer like this, the tower burned to the ground.'

'Burned . . .?' Mrs Phelps flinched.

'Hang on, that isn't all. A young girl is supposed to have died in the blaze. The old chap told a marvellous tale about how she was meeting her boyfriend there in secret and somehow the fire started, no one ever found out how, and the girl got trapped.'

'Don, listen . . .'

'The boyfriend ran off, scared he'd be caught with the girl, I expect. You know how strict they were in those days about that sort of thing, and quite right too. The wretched boy deserted her, poor thing, and she died in the flames. Young love betrayed by cowardice.'

'He's gone there,' Mrs Phelps said bleakly.

'A nice yarn but all nonsense, of course. However, it does look as if there might have been a tower somewhere

131

near where Martin thought he saw one. Isn't that odd!'

Mrs Phelps turned away and set off at a jog down the lane.

'Hang on, Mary,' Mr Phelps called after her, 'haven't finished yet.'

'Got to find him,' his wife called back.

'But wait!' Mr Phelps waved his stick. 'I want Martin to take us to where he thought he saw the tower.'

Without turning, Mrs Phelps shouted back, her voice carrying her panic, 'He's gone there already!'

Hearing at last what his wife was saying, Mr Phelps sprinted after her, ungainly in his walking boots. 'Gone there?' he called as he ran.

'To check. We must catch him.'

'Steady! Wait!' By the time Mr Phelps reached his wife he was almost speechless from lack of breath. He seized her arm and pulled her to a stop. 'Mary, you're being hysterical. What is all this?'

'Can't you see?' Mrs Phelps panted. 'Martin wasn't wrong!'

'Having us on!'

'No! There! To him, it was there!'

'Rubbish!' Mr Phelps leaned forward, both hands on his stick, recovering his breath. 'He'd found out. Only pretending he'd seen it. Some kind of joke.'

'*No, no, no!*' Mrs Phelps was near to tears with desperation.

Her husband glared at her. 'Pull yourself together, Mary, for heaven's sake!'

As if she had been slapped, his wife's tears suddenly gave way to anger. She glared fiercely back at her husband. 'Don't you speak to me like that, Don! You're not in school now! Don't you dare condescend to me! You think you know everything. To you the world is just one big museum of plain straightforward facts. Well, let me tell you, you don't know everything. There's more to this world than your boring facts! And for once I don't

132

care what you think. I believe Martin saw that tower. He's gone back there. And I'm going after him. I'm afraid what might happen if he sees it again. Call that a mother's intuition. Call it what you like. But I *feel* it. That's all I know. Now, are you coming or aren't you?'

Mr Phelps stood open-mouthed and rigid with astonishment at his wife's outburst.

By the time Martin reached the door of the tower smoke was billowing from every window and crevice. Instinctively bending almost double, he ran inside. The force of the air being sucked in through the doorway pressed against his bare back like a firm hand pushing him on. At once he found himself engulfed in blinding, choking fumes, could hear the roar of flames from across the room, could feel their blistering heat on his skin.

But still from above came the girl's panic-stricken cries.

Without thought or care, he threw himself to the left and on to the stairs. He pounded up them, stumbling, coughing. Hardly able to see for smoke, he kept his left hand pressed against the wall for fear of veering to the edge of the stairs and falling off into the furnace on the floor below, from where flames were already leaping high enough to lick the exposed floorboards of the room above. He held his right arm against his face, trying to protect it from the scorching blaze.

On the first floor flames were already eating at the boards. The dry wood was crackling; small explosions were sending showers of sparks cascading across the room. And, mingled with the suffocating fumes, the stench of burning flesh was so strong that Martin retched as he staggered on hands and feet now up the second flight of stairs. By the time he reached the trapdoor that gave on to the roof he was choking for breath, his smoke-filled eyes were streaming with tears and all down his right side he felt as if his skin were being peeled from him like paint being stripped by a blow-lamp.

The tower had become one giant, roaring chimney.

Martin hauled himself up into the air, gulping for breath. Once on the roof he clung for a moment to the parapet, unable to move till he recovered his strength. But he knew there was no time to spare. Through tear-blurred eyes and the fog of smoke swirling about him, he looked round for the girl and saw her only an arm's length away still waving and crying desperately in the direction of the road.

'Here!' he tried to shout, 'I'm here!', but the words clogged in his parched throat.

So he reached out to take her by the shoulders and turn her to him.

'Surely, we're nearly there!' Mrs Phelps panted.

Clumping along beside her, Mr Phelps, breathless too and sweating, said, 'That beech tree. Just there.'

Seconds later Mrs Phelps spotted her son's shirt and map lying abandoned in the road. 'Don!' she cried, rushed to them and picked them up. 'They're his!'

She turned and saw the gap in the hedge, and dashed towards it. But her husband, arriving at the same instant, pushed her aside and ran ahead into the field, causing Mrs Phelps to fall to her knees. 'Oh, God!' she pleaded, and, finding her feet again, stumbled after him.

'Martin . . .!' Mr Phelps was calling when both he and his wife were brought to a sudden stop.

Across the field, high above the pond, they saw their son floating upright in the air, his arms outstretched as if reaching for something.

'Dear Lord!' Mr Phelps muttered.

But neither he nor his wife could move. Spellbound, they could do no more than watch as their son took hold of that invisible something for which he was reaching and clutched it eagerly to him in a passionate embrace. For a long moment he remained like that, his body utterly still, until, suddenly, he opened his arms wide, peered down and, in a strangely slow, dream-like movement, as if from a high diving board, launched himself earthwards.

The instant Martin's body hit the water, Mrs Phelps came violently alive.

'Martin!' she screamed and hurtled across the field.

Her scream seemed to bring her husband back to his senses. He sprinted after her, yelling, 'Mary . . . Mary . . . Careful!'

But Mrs Phelps paid him no heed. By the time she reached the pond her son's body had surfaced and was floating face down in the middle. She plunged in headlong, her arms flaying, but found herself at once entangled in clinging weeds that grew around the edge and prevented her from making any progress.

Galloping up behind her, Mr Phelps made no attempt to swim, but ploughed in till he was wading waist-high towards his son, his frantic strides churning the water to froth around him and his boots so disturbing the stagnant mud on the pond's bottom that it belched up great bubbles of putrid gas in his trail.

As soon as they had lifted Martin on to the bank Mr Phelps said, 'Leave him to me!', and with a sureness and skill that surprised his wife, began reviving their son with the kiss of life.

It was only when Martin was breathing properly again that Mrs Phelps noticed the ugly blisters covering the right side of his body. She was sitting with Martin's head cradled in her lap and had been going to cover him with his shirt. Instead she looked at her husband who was kneeling at her side and saw that he too had seen the burns.

'We must get him to hospital,' she said, working hard to keep the shock from sounding in her voice.

Mr Phelps nodded.

Martin opened his eyes. 'Mum,' he said.

'Hush, sweetheart. It's all right. You're safe now.'

Martin blinked in the bright sunlight, and coughed up water. His mother eased his position, holding him so that he could breathe easily.

'Is the girl safe?' Martin asked when the spasm was over.

His parents glanced at each other.

'She'll be all right,' his mother said, smiling down at him.

Martin tried to raise himself. 'Where is she?' he asked.

His mother gently restrained him. 'She's been taken care of. Don't worry.'

'You see, Martin . . .' his father began.

'Not yet,' Mrs Phelps said as lightly as she could. 'Later.'

Her husband turned away. 'I'd better get the car and take you to hospital, old son,' he said.

Martin said, 'I told you it was there, Dad, didn't I?'

Mr Phelps peered across the empty field hidden from his son by his wife's cradling body.

'You did,' he said.

'And I got the position exactly on the map.'

'You certainly did. Well done!'

Mr Phelps looked down at his son and for a moment stared into his eyes for the first time in months. And the boy's gaze, looking frankly back at him, as though somehow he now knew all there was to know about his father, caused Mr Phelps to shudder.

Mrs Phelps observed her husband's discomfort and felt his pain. But there was nothing she could do to help him. The time for that had past. And their holiday too was over.

'We ought to get him away from here as soon as we can,' she said gently.

Mr Phelps took a deep breath and braced himself. 'I'll

only be a jiffy,' he said and set off towards the lane at a steady jog.

Mrs Phelps watched him go and suddenly felt utterly exhausted. The sun was scorching her back, but she knew she mustn't move. The warmth reminded her that Martin had said how cool it had been near the tower. It certainly wasn't now. And all around grasshoppers rasped. She listened. There was also plenty of bird noise and the loud skirl of passing flies and bees. None of the strange silence he'd mentioned.

Martin broke in on her thoughts. 'Am I badly hurt?'

'Not badly,' his mother said, brushing scorched hair from his forehead.

'Was I out for long?'

'Long enough.'

'Has the tower burned down completely?'

'Afraid so.'

'That's a pity. It was such a nice place. But the girl's OK?'

'I'm sure she is,' Mrs Phelps said with utter conviction. 'Thanks to you.'

'And I will see her again, won't I?'

'Would you like to?'

'Wouldn't mind.' Martin grinned sheepishly at his mother. 'She was quite pretty really.'

'Yes,' Mrs Phelps said, struggling against tears. 'I expect she was.'

Out of Time
Stories of the Future

A collection of science-fiction short stories by Joan Aiken, Ann Ruffell, Douglas Hill, Monica Hughes, Louise Lawrence, Christopher Leach, Jan Mark, Jill Paton Walsh and Robert Westall.

A Sporting Chance
Stories of Winning and Losing

Eight short stories by established authors including John Gordon, Jan Mark, Philippa Pearce, K. M. Peyton and Peggy Woodford, about young people taking a chance in life, set against a background of sport.